DEATH OUT OF NOWHERE

Locked Room
International

1

DEATH OUT OF NOWHERE

Alexis Gensoul & Charles Grenier

Translated by John Pugmire

Death out of Nowhere

First published in French in 1943 by
Editions S.T.A.E.L as *La Mort vient de nulle part*
Copyright © Editions S.T.A.E.L. 1943
DEATH OUT OF NOWHERE
English translation copyright © by John Pugmire 2019.

FIRST AMERICAN EDITION
Library of Congress Cataloguing-in-Publication Data
Gensoul, Alexis and Grenier, Charles
[*La Mort vient de nulle part* English]
Death out of nowhere/ Alexis Gensoul and Charles Grenier
Translated from the French by John Pugmire

CAST OF CHARACTERS

Hosts:
Baron Pierre de Malèves
Hélène de Malèves, his wife
Antoine de Malèves, their great-uncle

Guests:
Jeanne Féral, childhood friend of Hélène
Lucien Darlay, journalist
Jules Dublard, novelist
Louis Beaurieux, school supervisor
Yves Le Bellec, registration clerk

Servants:
Félix, the valet
Estelle, the cook
Léontine, the lady's maid
Gourvet, the gardener-caretaker
Pagnaud and his wife, farmers

and
Commissaire Machaux

The action takes place at the Breule Manor (Seine-et-Oise)

CONTENTS

I

Four friends in a roadhouse

They were inseparable friends, the four of them, gathered together in the small lodge of Breule Manor where, each year, Baron Pierre de Malèves offered them a peaceful and economical vacation.

The writer Jules Dublard was loudly describing the broad outlines of his forthcoming detective novel to his friends Beaurieux and Le Bellec; the third friend, the journalist Lucien Darlay, his nose buried in a comic book, appeared royally disinterested.

'This is the exact position of the corpse,' Dublard was saying, 'the feet under the Louis XV desk, and the head against the hearth. A Florentine dagger was planted between his shoulder blades. And, needless to say, the windows were locked and the door was bolted from the inside.'

'Why "needless to say"?' asked Le Bellec impudently.

Dublard looked indulgently at the questioner:

'Because it's the rule,' he explained. 'Haven't you ever read a detective novel? Anyone will tell you there are two schools: either the crime was committed in a hermetically sealed space, and one is left to wonder how the murderer did it; or, there's no sealed space, just a lot of people around, each more suspect than the rest, to the point that it's impossible to work out before the last page the name of the guilty party, chosen more or less artfully by the author.'

'And you,' chimed in Beaurieux, 'belong to the first school.'

'As you say. You can deduce it from what I've already written. Do you remember *The Bloody Slipper* and *Murder in the Basement*? Leave all those complicated plots, of which the reader quickly tires, to the English. As for me, I'm French and therefore Cartesian....'

'Bravo!' retorted Beaurieux. '"I think, therefore I am! "'

'Don't be an ass, you know very well what I mean, mister liberal arts graduate. One can be a humble writer of detective stories and still quote Descartes.'

Dublard raised his beer glass to his chin, looked around his small audience with satisfaction, and took a few sips. At thirty, he was already the proud possessor of a comfortable beer belly, and his crafty little eyes peered out of his moon face from under heavy lids. The rays of the setting sun caressed his forehead and gave his sparse blond hair the appearance of a halo, of the kind sported by stained-glass saints.

A splendid summer afternoon was ending. All around the little lodge, warm and glass-panelled like a greenhouse, extended the immaculately tended lawns of the property. Dublard, caressing his short moustache, considered the pink sky and the grey facade of the nearby manor through the bay window and gave a beatific smile, as if he himself were the owner of all he surveyed.

'Do you want a beer, Darlay?' asked Le Bellec.

'Thanks... not thirsty,' murmured the reporter.

'Leave him alone,' said Beaurieux. 'Someone must have told him that beer was fattening, and he wants to keep his figure.'

Meanwhile Dublard tried to regain the attention of his two friends.

'Forget about that,' he declared. 'Now I must reveal an extremely troubling detail. My corpse is holding in its clenched fingers... you'll never guess... the handle of a hurricane lamp!'

Le Bellec nodded solemnly, but Beaurieux, a decidedly more rebellious character, sneered:

'Pff!... I'd never have guessed... And why shouldn't it be holding a hurricane lamp?'

Dublard flinched at the remark. He became all commiseration:

'That's a point! I already explained that the corpse was that of a rich lawyer from Boulevard Saint-Germain. Wait! Le Bellec, you get it, don't you? The critical point of the puzzle: why would the lawyer be carrying a hurricane-lamp around his luxury flat at the very moment he's murdered?'

'That is a good point,' conceded Le Bellec.

'Good. I'm glad you agree. And if Beaurieux wasn't acting in such obvious bad faith, he would agree there was something infinitely troubling about it. '

'I don't find it troubling,' retorted Beaurieux, 'I find it idiotic. Do you get the subtle distinction?'

The words provoked a somewhat confused altercation. Dublard spluttered with indignation; Beaurieux continued to sneer; Le Bellec tried his best to calm things down. Eventually Dublard, who was too lazy to be angry for more than three minutes, waved away the objections and the sarcasm.

'That's okay. Let's just agree you're pig-headed and drop it. And anyway it was Le Bellec who asked me to tell him about my latest work. You needn't have listened if it bothered you. OK... roll of drums... Now we arrive at another curious point. There's another peculiar detail concerning the attitude of the corpse.'

'You're a pain in the neck with your corpse.'

This time the blow came from Darlay, who intervened without looking up from his comic book.

'Very well,' sighed Dublard, clearly dispirited by this new attack. 'I knock myself out to create jewels of ingenuity and cleverness, I ask my best friends to be my judge, and all I get in return is malice and incomprehension... It's true that I'm not a journalist at *L'Informateur* and I don't pride myself on my relations with the detective squad. Everything I write comes from the heart, which doesn't stop me from having quite a few readers prepared to buy my books.'

Darlay, impassive as ever, stretched out his legs on a chair and continued his reading with studied detachment. No one doubted he was secretly jubilant.

'I couldn't agree more,' said Beaurieux relentlessly, shaking his pipe. 'You're a real pain in the neck with your corpse. It's always the same thing you serve up, with a different dressing each time—just like all your colleagues, by the way. Bright sparks, all of you. You decide the denouement before you start the story... You put together snippets of mystery, studiously withholding any details which would allow your readers to work out the solution for themselves. When the joke has gone on long enough, you end the story with two shakes of a lamb's tail and casually write "THE END" at the bottom of the one-hundred-and-eighty-first page....'

'Uh-oh!' exclaimed Le Bellec, amused but anxious.

'I'm willing to bet a hundred francs that you have no idea, as we speak, how your murderer is going to get out of the room.'

'You lose!' announced Dublard triumphantly. 'I know perfectly well how he gets out. I just haven't decided how he gets in... But I'll let you know that tomorrow. Now what have you left to sneer about?'

Beaurieux rocked gently backwards and forwards on his chair. He was a dreamer and a freckled redhead who turned up his nose at the daily complications of life. He turned to look nonchalantly at Darlay.

'Did you hear that? He asked me why I sneer! I don't like theoreticians, that's all! They live in an imaginary world, fabricated to their whim. I smile at the thought of our Dublard faced with a real crime and no doubt with less perspicacity than a village constable.'

'You can always rant on in bad faith, as usual. I'm not a commisssaire (1) or an inspecteur from the Sûreté, so it's unlikely I shall ever have the opportunity to exercise my skills and make you eat your words.'

Dublard served himself another beer. He was happy to have shown that, despite his earlier outburst, he was indeed capable of self-control. Suddenly his manner became suave.

'Mademoiselle!' he exclaimed. 'I drink to your health!'

A beautiful girl had appeared in the doorway of the lodge, her tall athletic figure, with its elegant curves, framed against the sun.

'Thank you, Monsieur Dublard,' she replied with a smile.

'A glass of beer, Mademoiselle?' asked Le Bellec.

'Yes, if you please... How is it, Messieurs, that you're all caged up inside here, and all I'm left with for company on my walk is Mister Buck!'

'Upon my word, Mademoiselle Féral,' replied Beaurieux impertinently, 'you'll have to excuse us. We can't help it. Even in the countryside, we can't shake the habit. Here we are, all four of us, inside the lodge, just as we are three or four times a week at the same time at "Chez Marcel," near the mairie (2) of the IXth district. And, just as back there, we're drinking whilst discussing matters of no consequence.'

'That's perfectly true,' said Dublard. 'Exactly like "Chez Marcel," only with nature added.'

'Our host would be enormously flattered to hear the comparison,' the girl replied teasingly.

'To a bistro?' said Beaurieux. 'Bah! Pierre has known for a long time. Don't forget we've been coming here for six years. By the way, miss, this edifice was once known, architecturally speaking, as a "roadhouse." We are restoring it to its rightful role.'

(1) Superintendent   (2) Town hall

'Six years in a row... what consistency and friendship.'

'Certainly,' agreed Beaurieux. 'It's that above everything else. And besides, Dublard, how is it that you spend your vacations in Seine-et-Oise instead of pampering yourself on the Côte d'Azur?'

'Huh?' choked Dublard.

'Likewise. With my teaching salary at Louis-le-Grand, can you imagine me swanning around down there? Le Bellec, it must be out of vice....'

'Oh!' choked Le Bellec.

'These clerks are repressed individuals. Not to mention Darlay. One mustn't speak ill of the absent.'

'Hum,' grunted the journalist, his nose still in the comic book.

'And there you are,' concluded Beaurieux, shaking his red mop. 'You heard the outpouring of eloquence.'

'I heard,' said the girl, with a note of irony in her voice. 'Continue, gentlemen, I'll resume my solitary walk.'

Darlay intervened gallantly:

'If you will allow me, Mademoiselle, I can replace Mister Buck.'

'There... That surprised me as well,' said Dublard.

'What surprised you?' asked the journalist.

'That you didn't move when there was a member of the weaker sex in the vicinity.'

'Idiot.'

Mister Buck, the fox terrier, had jumped on a spare chair and was watching them friskily, as if part of the conversation.

'They're boring,' continued the journalist. 'All they talk about is corpses. It's irritating when one is reading about the flora of Haut-Oubangi.'

'Brr....' said Jeanne Féral. 'Let's leave, Monsieur Darlay. Would you like to go as far as the farm?'

***

'What's the matter with you tonight?' murmured Le Bellec to Beaurieux. 'You're very aggressive this evening. First Dublard, then Mademoiselle Féral.'

'Forget it,' replied Beaurieux.

And, grabbing Le Bellec by the wrist, he whispered, in a tragic voice which contrasted with his gracious smile:

'I don't know what's got into me, my old friend. It's weird. All of a sudden, *I feel like killing someone.*'

II

The Emperor of China's coup

Twilight was falling. All around the lodge, the park was fading into soft colours. Dublard watched the receding figures distractedly, then emptied the bottle into his glass.

'What about me?' protested Le Bellec.

'There's another in the corner... What are you looking for, Beaurieux?'

'The pack of cards.'

'Over there, on the table. Do you want to play *écarté*?'

'No, but I need the cards. Say, Le Bellec, have you seen the red mat?'

'There's one over there.'

'No, not the blue one. I need a red one.'

'What difference does it make?' grumbled Dublard. 'Does the blue tire your eyes? Anyway, the red one's underneath you.'

He pointed to the other's posterior.

'Don't mind me.'

'That way you're depriving yourself.'

'Yes, but not the red one. Dublard, my good friend, make an effort, stand up; give me the red mat... Here's the blue one in exchange.'

'You're annoying,' said Dublard, getting up nevertheless.

Beaurieux drew up a chair and sat down on the red mat.

'Suppose I took you at your word?' he asked Dublard abruptly.

'About what?'

'You say you don't get the chance to display your talents... Would you like me to give you an opportunity?'

Dublard shrugged without deigning to reply; one always had to be suspicious of Beaurieux's bluster.

'Don't give me that disdainful look. I assure you, I'm serious. You keep talking about the perfect crime... the famous crimes found in the annals of justice and, above all, in the rantings of types like you... The beautiful crime committed by a master who has taken every

15

precaution not to leave the slightest trace... Suppose I offer you one now? Do you feel up to the task of showing how it was done?'

'Ah! Ah! When did this masterpiece take place? What old case are you going to rake up from newspaper clippings?'

'Not old at all, my boy... I'll tell you.'

Beaurieux leant across the table confidentially.

'Just to be more precise, *it's a crime in the future*, a very powerful one, do you understand?'

'Well, that's very interesting. How nice of you to warn me!'

Dublard was happy to play the game. He considered himself to be every bit as intelligent as Beaurieux. He could swap nonsense with him for hours on end.

'I'll tell you now, so you won't quibble about it later: you'll know everything you need to know. Usually, by the time an investigator gets involved, some time has gone by since the crime was committed... and the murderer is unknown, or has disappeared. What I'm proposing is that *you fix the time of the crime*, and I'll name the culprit in advance.'

'Who will be...?'

'Me, for heaven's sake!'

'Hey, wait a minute,' exclaimed Le Bellec in mock outrage, and pretending to be about to flee. 'You're not going to play me a dirty trick, just for the fun of annoying Dublard.'

Beaurieux calmed him with a dignified gesture:

'Don't worry, the crime won't happen here, and you won't suffer; otherwise, what would be the point? I'm simply saying to Dublard: at an hour of your choosing, I shall commit a perfect crime. It will be up to you to explain how I did it, and to furnish sufficient proof of my guilt. Are we in agreement?'

Dublard was starting to get irritated:

'You find this amusing? Well, I'm game. Go ahead.'

'All of a sudden, just like that?'

'You said I could choose the time, and I've chosen it. Go ahead. Don't be shy.'

'You'll let me have five minutes grace, all the same? You've caught me a bit short.'

Dublard opened his arms wide in a gesture of magnanimity.

'Granted.'

'Very well. What time is it now?'

'Quarter-past seven,' announced Le Bellec, holding his watch up. 'Or, if you want to be official about it, nineteen hours, fifteen minutes.'

'And what time do you show, Dublard?'

'The same. You made us synchronise our watches earlier, in your room.'

'I remember. With the alarm clock on my dresser. At that time I was already out of the room and in the hallway, and it was you who shut the door.'

'That's right. What's your point?'

'So that there's absolutely no doubt about the time the crime will be committed. Hell's bells! I only have three minutes left. Let's go....'

Quickly, Beaurieux took out his handkerchief, tied a knot on each of the four corners, and placed the improvised bonnet on his head. Le Bellec started to slap himself on the thighs.

'Ha, Ha! What a clown!'

But the other, as solemn as a pope, picked up the pack of cards and spread it out on the mat. He selected three and named them:

'The ace of hearts... king of spades... ace of diamonds.'

Setting the rest aside, he left the three cards on the mat, the king between the two aces.

'There's one minute left,' he said. 'There's still time to stop, Dublard.'

'Cretin!' exclaimed Dublard.

'On your head be it, then. Watch carefully: nothing in my hands, nothing in my pockets....'

Suddenly, he picked up the king of spades and threw it on the floor.

'And the Emperor of China be damned!' he proclaimed loudly.

Dublard, scornfully, and Le Bellec, mockingly, waited to see what happened next, but Beaurieux calmly folded the red mat.

'There,' he concluded. 'I assume my alibi is sound.'

'That's all?'

'Yes, that's all. Now it's up to you, Dublard, old boy. In a few seconds it'll happen. I'll tell you right now, it will occur in the south wing of the manor. Method Dublard, of course. Doors and windows hermetically closed, a single revolver shot. Listen carefully, my lad.'

'May I pick up the king of spades?' asked Le Bellec, somewhat impressed.

'Yes... Shh!'

Beaurieux went over to the half-open bay window and listened, his finger in the air.

'Ah! Good grief!' exclaimed Le Bellec, with a start.

A detonation shattered the calm, somewhere in the direction of the manor....

***

'I don't think there's much left for us to do here,' said Beaurieux.

'Not so fast ,' grumbled Dublard. 'You gave the gardener's son a franc to let off a firework at the appointed hour. I'm not that stupid.'

'My little Dublard, you should know that a good detective is wary of preconceived ideas. Why don't we go over to the scene of the crime?'

'Why not?' asked Le Bellec, 'Particularly since it must be nearly dinner time.'

'Well spoken!' exclaimed Dublard. 'All your nonsense has made me hungry; we'll look into the crime after the dessert.'

'Suit yourself.'

The three friends set off. A winding path led from the roadhouse to the manor, between the undergrowth and the French garden with its ornamental lake. As they started to climb the small flight of steps up to the terrace, a shrill cry rang out from a wide-open window on the upper floor.

III

A really obscure tragedy

Darlay and Mlle. Féral had returned to the manor after a relatively brief walk in the park. The three other guests having not yet arrived, they decided to go to their respective rooms to freshen up before the evening meal. On reaching the upper floor landing, they could see Félix the valet knocking nervously on the door of M. Antoine de Malèves's bedroom.

'What's wrong, Félix?' asked the journalist. 'You seem upset.'

The valet gave a slight jump, not having heard Mlle. Féral and the journalist approaching. But he recovered immediately:

'I don't think so...,' he began.

'What don't you think?'

'My goodness, Monsieur, maybe I shouldn't be anxious, but a few seconds ago I thought I heard moans coming from Monsieur Antoine's room... followed by a noise which sounded like a body falling... And the uncle of Monsieur le Baron isn't responding...'

Darlay came closer and knocked on the door himself.

'Monsieur de Malèves,' he called out twice.

The call was in vain.

'Uh, oh!' he said. 'That's strange... Are you sure Monsieur Antoine is in there?'

'Quite sure, Monsieur.'

Pierre de Malèves arrived, attracted by the noise.

'What's happening, Darlay?'

The journalist brought him up to speed. He, too, tried to open the door.

'My uncle is obviously indisposed,' he said. 'We'll have to break the door down.'

Darlay nodded. Pierre de Malèves put his shoulder to the door panel. At the third attempt, the door gave way.

The three men stood in the doorway for a moment. M. Antoine de Malèves was stretched out, face down, on the floor, his head next to

19

the desk and right arm folded behind his back. The journalist was the first to approach him. He bent over the old man. When he stood up again, he made a vague gesture to indicate nothing could be done.

Mlle. Jeanne Féral, who had stayed in the corridor and observed the scene with horrified eyes, realised that death had done its work. She emitted a cry of distress and fled the scene.

But Darlay, intrigued, seemed to be looking for something. He turned to Félix:

'Phone the gendarmerie,' he said. 'Tell them it's urgent... There's been a crime....'

The valet ran down the stairs helter-skelter.

'But why?' asked Pierre.

Darlay showed him a small tear above the victim's belt, close to his right hand. He touched it with his finger.

'You see? It's blood... there's a bullet in there. And I heard a shot a short while ago. There's no weapon in the room. That means....'

He stopped. In shock, he looked at the window. He went over for a closer look; it was closed, as were the metal shutters. Next, he went to the door and examined the lock. The bolt was shut, but under the blows from Pierre de Malèves' shoulder, the strike plate had given way.

'I'll be damned,' he murmured.

The single light bulb which illuminated the room was on.

Dublard, Beaurieux and Le Bellec arrived on the scene.

'What's happened?' asked the novelist. 'We heard a cry.'

He started into the room, followed by the two others. Darlay stopped him:

'Monsieur de Malèves has been murdered. It's best not to touch anything, or even remain here. Stay in the corridor.'

He explained how he'd discovered the crime.

'What's inexplicable,' he added, 'is that Monsieur de Malèves had locked himself in. The door was locked and the window and shutters are closed.'

'Maybe he....' began Le Bellec.

Darlay understood that his friend was thinking of suicide. He shrugged his shoulders:

'There's no weapon anywhere near him ... And the bullet is in his back, below the belt.'

20

Pierre, his eyes fixed on his uncle's body, was aghast. Le Bellec shot Beaurieux a strange look, which Dublard noticed. He was just about to say something when steps were heard on the staircase. The gendarmes had arrived, preceded by Félix.

After having asked his friends to take Pierre de Malèves away and look after him, Darlay had a brief conversation with the brigadier (1). The latter proceeded to carry out a thorough examination of the premises. When he had finished, he made no attempt to conceal his perplexity.

'It's quite extraordinary!' he exclaimed.

In the hours that followed, he questioned the servants and all the guests who were in the manor at the time of the incident. Then he phoned Le Parquet (2) at Versailles.

'Commissaire Machaux will be here tomorrow morning,' he said on his return.

'Perfect,' replied the journalist. 'I know him well.'

It was very late, but no one had thought about dinner. Only Dublard had gone to the kitchen on his way to his room, to ask Estelle to make him a large sandwich.

(1) Sergeant (2) Public prosecutor

IV

Darlay expounds

Darlay and Commissaire Machaux were seated in the smoking-room, where large armchairs invited laziness.

'Cigarette?' offered the policeman.

'No thanks. I was smoking all night. My mouth is dry from nicotine.'

Commissaire Machaux, of the Police judiciare (1), had arrived early in the morning, accompanied by an assistant from the police laboratory. He was pleased to find the journalist Lucien Darlay, whom he had known for a long time, at the scene of the crime. He had immediately cornered him, confident that he would get a clear picture of what had happened and useful information about the other actors who had lived through the tragedy.

The policeman, who had had some difficulty in lighting a cigarette with a rebellious lighter, settled comfortably in his armchair.

He was a tall man, well-dressed, but with a distant manner. His tone of studied nonchalance was deceptive, as Darlay knew only too well; where necessary, Machaux was not afraid to put his life on the line.

'I wanted to spend a few minutes with you, my dear friend,' he declared. 'I haven't forgotten, believe me, our little collaboration during the case of double murder in Saint-Cyr.'

'Quite little, in fact....'

'Come now, old friend, you're a good man. You're not troublesome, unlike most of your colleagues, who shall remain nameless. You don't say much and only talk about what's strictly necessary. But a well-chosen phrase is worth more than a long discourse. I remember that article in *L'Informateur*. It was short, but it contained three lines which worried the culprit and caused him to reveal himself through sheer carelessness. So, I'm pleased to see you again.'

(1) Detective Division

23

'You're too kind. But I must point out that I'm here as the guest of a dear friend, and so....'

'Another good reason! I'm not asking you as journalist... It's just that, as you well know, I got here a bit late: one night after the actual incidents, which is hardly ideal. It's all the fault of the Alvarez affair... It's all hands on deck, and Monsieur Manceau, the juge d'instruction (1) hasn't left Versailles. It's a miracle they found anyone to send here... And, according to the brigadier's report, this business isn't at all clear. Or maybe it's all too clear: there's no explanation! It's a mystifying report.'

'Don't blame the gendarmes,' replied Darlay. 'They did their best; but they were working in a void. There's a victim and a wound, and that's all. The witnesses' depositions: they're non-existent. The motive for the crime: it's completely unknown. The circumstances of the crime: there aren't any. What do you expect the sergeant to say?'

Machaux tried to light his cigarette again, but Darlay didn't have any matches and the lighter refused to work. The commissaire began to dismantle it.

'So,' he said eventually, 'we're starting from scratch and waiting for the médecin légiste's (2) report. Well, that does have its advantages. Let's start to lay the groundwork. I'll summarize.

'Yesterday evening, around seven-twenty, a shot rang out, heard by several witnesses. A servant who happened to be passing by Monsieur Antoine de Malèves' room hears moans and a body falling. He tries to open the door, but it's bolted from the inside. He calls for help. The door is broken down and they find a body. Death was from a bullet in the back. No weapon was found in the room, and a quick look determined that suicide was impossible. Now, aside from the door, the only connection to the outside world is a window whose metal shutters are firmly locked and whose panes of glass are intact. There's no fireplace. No disorder, no sign of a struggle. That's it.'

'As you say, that's it.'

The lighter had been reassembled. A flame shot out at the first attempt; the commissaire's face wore the satisfaction of someone who has accomplished a tricky operation.

'We can now approach the problem in two ways: study the crime

(1) examining magistrate   (2) medical examiner

24

itself and try to work out how it could have been committed, which could lead us to the murderer; or look at the motives which might have led to the crime, by familiarising ourselves with the atmosphere inside the manor and the personalities of its inhabitants. That's where I'm going to start. I think it'll be easier. That's where I believe you can be very useful to me by describing what you know about each of them. That way, when I start to take their testimony, I'll already know a little bit about them. Now, my friend, let's hear from you.'

Darlay, his chin resting on the palm of his hand, began:

'I've known Baron Pierre de Malèves, the master of the house, for eight or nine years. We became friends at the Law Faculty in Paris, where we were both studying for our licence. When I say studying... I soon switched to journalism. As for Pierre, he was the most charming of friends, but the laziest of students. He was basically an amateur... In the course of the two years, whilst we were cementing our friendship, Pierre, whose mother was already deceased, lost his father as well... His fortune allowed him to renounce his studies. He married shortly afterwards. Madame de Malèves, the daughter of a colonial administrator, is as friendly as she is distinguished.'

'Was it a marriage of love?'

'What do you mean?'

'Any children?'

'No. Or rather one, in a way.'

'What do you mean, one?'

'Uncle Antoine... or great-uncle, to be precise. An old gentleman who has spent his entire life here in the manor, taking care of his collections of butterflies or stamps, gentle and carefree, blessed by a fate which allowed him to avoid life's difficulties, which he would have been utterly incapable of handling.'

'No dissension of any kind?'

'Not the slightest hint... the charming old fellow was spoilt by everyone around him, and particularly his niece, whom he adored. Any thoughts of vengeance on her part are out of the question.'

'And what about any inheritance?'

'You'd have to ask someone more in the know. However, I do believe that Antoine de Malèves, who was inept at running his affairs, had lost a lot of money in the past. Even so, he couldn't have been much of a burden for his well-to-do nephews, as you must already be aware.'

The commissaire jotted some notes down in a little black book.

'No other family members living here?'

'No. You'll need to examine the guests and the servants.'

'The guests being?'

'Five in all. Mademoiselle Jeanne Féral, a childhood friend of Madame de Malèves and, like her, the daughter of a colonial administrator, but now an orphan, I believe... and penniless. Here since four or five weeks ago. Returned from Indochina last year.'

'What's your impression?'

'Oh, a very nice girl, a trifle independent, like most women brought up outside France. Gets on well with everyone.'

'Very well. And now you?'

'Me, multiplied by four.'

'Sorry?

Darlay smiled:

'I mean there are four of us. Apart from yours truly, there's a school supervisor, a writer of detective novels, and a registration clerk. A strange bunch, eh?'

'I didn't say a word.'

'And we're all on familiar terms with the Baron de Malèves, a descendant of the Crusaders. We met in Paris. We formed a little club where everyone gets on swimmingly, despite social standing or professional situation. And it's still going on... Pierre de Malèves is a really nice chap. The four of us are more or less without family, and, so far, fortune hasn't smiled upon us; so, every summer we have our "season" here, rich and happy, stocking up on fresh air and the courage to face the rest of the year.'

'And, needless to say, your friends are also nice chaps.'

'Naturally.'

'Very well. And what about the servants?'

'The gardener-caretaker, Gourvet, is the baron's foster brother. Félix, the valet, and Estelle, the cook, have been here since time immemorial. The lady's maid, Léontine, is a niece of the cook. All of them are devoted body and soul to their masters, which is rather rare.'

'What you're telling me is quite disturbing!'

'You're joking.'

'Not at all. I come here to investigate a murder and I find myself in the middle of one of the Comtesse de Ségur's books... The hosts are charming, the friends are all loyal, the servants are above suspicion, and I assume you're ready to vouch for all of them!'

Darlay, looking very serious, thought hard for a few seconds.

'Yes, really. I hardly slept last night, so I had time to think it all over. There are only two people here that I can't vouch for personally, because I don't know them well enough: Mademoiselle Féral and the little lady's maid. Not to mention that the circumstances of the case seem to rule out every one of the residents, no matter who.'

'So, according to you, a stranger....'

Darlay folded his arms:

'I didn't say that: I'm just going to limit myself to a few observations. This murder is so out of the ordinary that I'm unwilling to offer any hypothesis whatsoever.'

Machaux got up and, looking preoccupied, started to pace up and down the room.

'As you wish. But before I start my interrogations, would you be good enough to provide me with a plan of the property?'

'That's easy enough... I'll give you one of the ground floor and one of the upper floor.'

'What's that?' asked Machaux. 'The circle you've drawn opposite the southern extremity?'

'It's a dovecote. You must have noticed it when you first arrived.'

'Yes, I remember it perfectly. It looks ancient.'

'It is indeed. It's a very old tower, the only remains of a castle built in the Middle Ages, slightly to the east of what you see now, which dates from the seventeenth century and was capped by a circular roof in order to serve as a dovecote. But there haven't been any birds there for a very long time.'

'How far is it from the manor? Ten, fifteen metres? It seems quite close.'

'About fifteen metres. One gets the impression the architect didn't have much room to manoeuvre. He had to foreshorten the south wing in order to respect the tower, then had to do the same for the north wing for the sake of symmetry. As a result, they both look incomplete, which mars the appearance of the otherwise beautiful manor....

27

Upper Floor

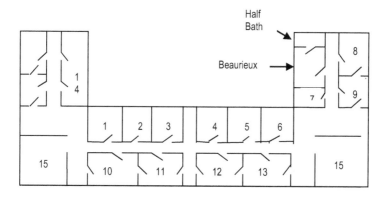

1 = Empty	9 = Boudoir
2 = Small salon	10 = Pierre de Malèves
3 = Darlay	11 = Study
4 = Le Bellec	12 = Boudoir
5 = Dublard	13 = Hélène de Malèves
6 = Antoine de Malèves	14 = Linen Room
7 = Bathroom	15 = Staircase
8 = Jeanne Féral	16 = Tower

'Wait a minute. I know what you're thinking.'

'I didn't say a word.'

'I know, but you need to know that you can't see Antoine de Malèves' room from the tower. The south wing blocks the view.'

'Bravo!' replied Machaux with a smile. 'I can see we're going to make a great team, my policeman-journalist. We've set the scene. Now let's see the cast of characters, starting with your good self. Have you an alibi?'

'Yes, my dear fellow, and I consider it to be perfect.'

'I'm very suspicious of perfect alibis, as you know.'

'Too bad. I spent a good part of the afternoon in that lodge which you can see from here, in the company of friends: Beaurieux....'

'The novelist?'

'No, the school supervisor. Dublard is the novelist and Le Bellec is the registration clerk. Mademoiselle Féral stopped by at around seven o'clock. I left my companions in order to accompany the young lady; we walked together as far as the entrance to the park, where we chatted for a while with Gourvet. We walked over to the manor via a small detour and, just as we reached the terrace, we heard the shot. It was twenty-past seven.'

'Did you get the impression that the shot came from inside the manor?'

'I really can't say,' replied the journalist, weighing his words. 'It wasn't muffled, but several windows were open on the upper floor, which doesn't prove anything, one way or the other. Nonetheless, it seemed to come from relatively far away... as if from a room on the other side of the manor, or the adjacent park. It seemed to fall out of the sky.'

'What did you do?'

'Well, nothing. I didn't think at the time that it was anything serious. I was in a lively discussion with Mademoiselle Féral and I didn't pay it much attention. Pierre sometimes amuses himself by firing at crows in the old lime trees, who annoy everyone with the noise they make. We entered the manor via the short flight of steps and took the south staircase to get to our rooms.

'When we reached the upper floor, we saw the valet Félix banging on Antoine de Malèves' door, trying to rouse him. He told me that, as he was going past the door, he heard a deep thud and moaning noises.

29

He thought the old man had been taken ill. Félix hadn't heard the shot and I didn't remember it just then. Just then Pierre de Malèves arrived along the corridor via the north staircase. After a short discussion we decided to break the door down. As soon as we were inside, we could see he was dead, and I told the others not to touch anything.'

'Needless to say, the shutters were closed and the electricity was working?'

'Yes. As you must have noticed, the room was devoid of luxury. Antoine de Malèves was a man of simple tastes. There's just a single light bulb hanging above the desk.'

'But it wasn't dark yet, was it?'

'No, but the old man's eyesight wasn't good and Félix was in the habit of closing the shutters and turning on the light as soon as it started to get dark.'

'The gendarmes arrived half an hour later, I believe?'

'Roughly. There's a telephone here.'

'Very well. I can't think of anything else to ask, for the moment. I'm going to ask the Baron de Malèves....'

Darlay stood up as if to leave, but Machaux bade him stay:

'No, you can stay. That should make my task easier.'

He rang for Félix and asked him to fetch his master.

V

Did Félix lie?

Pierre de Malèves came in, and the policeman had the same thought as when the lord of the manor had greeted him:
"You can't judge a book by its cover... appearances can be deceptive."
Before him was a shortish, ruddy-cheeked man, embarrassed by his hands and the rest of his person, dressed in a drab hunting outfit and wearing heavy boots: he looked for all the world like a farmer visiting his landowner. He coughed slightly to attract attention; his rather bulging eyes darted anxiously from Darlay to the superintendent.

'Did you wish to see me?' he asked, with some effort.

'Please take a seat, Monsieur,' said Machaux. ("Hell's bells. Which one of us is in his own home?" he thought.) I'd be obliged if we could go over a few details. I assume the presence of Mr. Darlay doesn't bother you?'

'On the contrary,' replied de Malèves. 'I'm sure... I'd like....'

'Listen, Pierre,' interrupted the journalist bluntly, 'sit down. Have you any cigarettes? I've been telling the superintendent what a decent chap you are. He has a splendid estate, you know,' he continued, addressing the policeman, 'and all under his direction.'

'It's you who are the decent chap, Lucien....' There was a warm look of friendship and confidence in his eyes which transfigured him. 'It's true that I have a tendency to mumble. I'm at your disposal, superintendent, if I can be of assistance.'

'Thank you. This won't take long. Have you any thoughts about last night's incident?'

'None. I'm at a loss to conjecture. It's incomprehensible.'

'Nobody, according to you, would have any reason to....'

'Nobody, Monsieur; my uncle was the most inoffensive of men. It's impossible to conceive of any vengeance towards him, and I can't think of any other motive.'

'Do you trust your servants?'

31

'Absolutely... They've all been here a long time except Léontine, the lady's maid, and I've known her since she was born.'

'You were moving about quite a bit yesterday afternoon, I believe. Did you notice anything out of the ordinary?'

'Nothing. Just like any other day, I did my tour of the estate. They're ploughing at this time of year, and I was coming back from the farm at about a quarter-past seven.'

'Your farmers?'

'An old family in the region, the Pagnauds. Solid people.'

'Your agricultural hands?'

'Three, all from around here. Two of them are married.'

'As you were saying, you were returning at around quarter-past seven....'

'Yes, the farm's about three hundred metres away. I cut through the woods and approached the manor from the north side.'

'That's the wing away from the tower,' explained Darlay.

'I was still about fifty metres away when I heard a detonation. I was astonished....'

'Where did the shot appear to come from?'

'From my left, in other words from the south side of the manor, but I can't say exactly where... I came in by the side door and went up the stairs. I was going to see my wife, who's been confined to her room for the last two days.'

'Madame de Malèves is indisposed?'

'Oh, nothing serious; she gets migraine attacks from time to time. As I reached the upper floor landing, I saw a group of people outside my uncle's door. There were Mademoiselle Féral, Darlay and Félix. I approached—.'

At that moment there was a knock on the door. The lord of the manor stopped.

'It's me, Dumain,' said a deep voice.

'Come in, doctor,' replied Machaux. 'I shan't be needing you any more, Monsieur,' he continued, talking to Pierre... 'If you have business to attend to....'

Docteur Dumain closed the door on the departing figure. Still young, he sported the classical beard and lorgnettes. He was carrying a compress.

'Well, Docteur?' asked Machaux.

'Here's the bullet,' replied the médecin légiste.

'Perfect. It was....'

'In the right kidney; more precisely, the hilus: the renal artery was severed, causing internal haemorrhage... Death was almost immediate. The shot was fired at a slightly downward angle and certainly from a distance, because despite only touching soft parts, it didn't seem to penetrate with much force.'

The policeman thought for a moment.

'Suppose someone fired from the south landing....'

'I don't think so,' said the médecin légiste firmly. 'That would mean seven or eight metres maximum. You can see the bullet... it looks as though it came from a heavy service pistol, or something of the sort.'

'Very well. Any other observations?'

'Nothing of note. I'll go and write up my report. The body is in the bottom room of the tower, where I did the autopsy, if you want to see it.'

'Maybe. In any case, I'll see you this evening.'

***

The valet was standing rigidly to attention before the policeman, as if on guard duty; his fingers were trembling slightly. He was already an old man.

'My name is Félix Desplanches, Monsieur le juge, and I'm fifty-seven years old.'

'Very well, my friend, but I'm not a juge... only a commissaire... You've been a servant in the Breule manor for quite a long time, I believe?'

'Twenty-one years, Monsieur le commissaire. I've watched Monsieur le Baron grow up, you might say.'

'Very well. Needless to say, I have a few questions for you... You closed the shutters in the victim's room every night, didn't you?'

'That is so.'

'Was Monsieur Antoine usually in the room then?'

'Generally speaking, yes. I always went before nightfall; I knocked, and if Monsieur Antoine wasn't there, I went in and closed the shutters, which is what happened yesterday evening. I knew that

Ground Floor

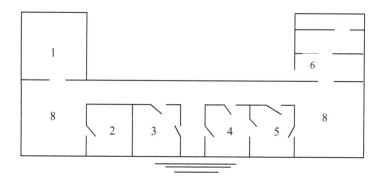

1 = Billiard Room
2 = Library
3 = Salon
4 = Smoking Room
5 = Dining Room
6 = Kitchen
7 = Tower
8 = Staircase

Monsieur Antoine was in the library. The evenings he was in his room, he opened the door for me, because he always locked himself in.'

'Why, do you know?'

'Monsieur Antoine was a bit... fussy. An old man, as Monsieur Darlay can confirm.'

'That's true,' said Darlay, who had been keeping to his corner of the room.

'And what did you do after that?'

'I went downstairs and tidied up the smoking room, then I laid out the settings in the dining room; after that, I went upstairs again to get a clean apron from the linen room. As I was going up, I looked through the French window and saw Monsieur Darlay and Mademoiselle Féral arriving at the terrace.'

'We'd just heard the detonation,' observed the journalist.

Félix shook his head.

'I didn't hear anything at all. I climbed the stairs; I remember stopping at the top to tie a shoelace... then I took the corridor because the linen-room was at the other end. As I went past Monsieur Antoine's door, I heard moans and a thud... obviously the poor gentleman falling down... That's when Monsieur Darlay arrived.'

'In other words,' said the policeman, after Félix had left the room, 'we know for certain that Antoine de Malèves wasn't killed immediately... He survived during the time it took for Félix to reach the upper floor and tie his shoelace. Let's say thirty or forty seconds... Which really doesn't help very much.'

***

Estelle, the cook, solidly-built and ruddy-faced, came in next, bringing with her the aromas of a herb garden. Armed with a clear conscience and voluble, she announced that her name was Estelle Rangeon, she was forty-six years old, and had worked in the manor for seventeen years. She hadn't left her kitchen between six o'clock and the discovery of the poor old gentleman.

Machaux peered at Darlay's plan.

'Kitchen?'

'Here,' said the journalist. 'The office occupies the entire ground floor of the south wing. It's comprised of three parts: the kitchen, near the staircase, then the servants' dining area, and finally the pantry, in the part closest to the tower.'

Estelle had clearly heard the detonation:

'When I say detonation,' she said, shrugging her shoulders, 'that's what everyone's calling it... but it really doesn't deserve to be called that.'

'What?' exclaimed Machaux in astonishment. 'It was heard from more than a hundred and fifty metres by some witnesses! What was it then?'

Waving her hands, the fat Estelle looked up to the sky and tried to think.

'Wait... let's see... yes, that's it! You know when little boys amuse themselves by blowing into a paper bag and bursting it against a wall? Well, it was just like that, I can't describe it better.'

'Maybe you were badly placed to hear it clearly?'

'Oh, no!' replied the cook calmly. 'I was quite close, I'm sure. I was preparing feed for the chickens. I was turning the handle, which makes quite a noise... While I was resting for a few seconds, I heard the noise clearly. I even looked towards the window.'

'Which window?'

'The one facing inwards.'

'Towards Monsieur Antoine's room?'

'Yes, but this was at ground level and not far from me, as I said. I didn't pay much attention, I kept grinding the meat. Félix came into the kitchen.'

Machaux looked startled:

'Are you sure Félix came in after you heard the noise?'

'Oh, yes. Maybe a quarter of a minute afterwards. He wanted a clean apron. He stayed a little while chatting, then I sent him to the linen room.'

'What do you mean by a little while?'

'Maybe a minute.'

'Did you talk to him about the detonation?'

'Not for the life of me, it was such a little thing!'

***

'Let's see,' said Machaux, after the cook had left. 'There's something not quite right. Could Félix have seen you before you arrived at the terrace with Mademoiselle Féral?'

'No,' replied Darlay. 'There are spindle trees hiding the path. Besides, Félix made it clear that we were on the terrace: we'd already heard the detonation clearly.'

'So, Félix is mistaken or lying... He claims to have seen you whilst going upstairs to get his apron, in other words after he'd been to the kitchen and more than a minute after Estelle had heard the detonation. Or else you and Madmoiselle Féral stayed more than a minute at the top of the terrace steps.'

'No,' said the reporter, 'we didn't stop, and it only takes a few seconds to go from that staircase to the side steps.'

'So, Félix has been pulling the wool over our eyes.'

'Unless...,' said the journalist slowly, his head in his hands.

'Unless?'

'There were two detonations.'

The policeman looked doubtful.

'Separated by an interval of approximately a minute and a half,' continued Darlay. 'The cook was the only one to hear the first, which she said was not very loud. That doesn't mean there wasn't another, heard by other witnesses.'

'Which Estelle didn't hear....'

'She was operating her mincing machine,' the journalist pointed out.

'Hell's bells,' said the superintendent, looking at his watch. 'Time flies. If I want to look around the grounds... I would have liked to get to the bottom of these detonations, and there are other witnesses to question.'

'Maybe, whilst you're waiting for that opportunity, I could tell you what I've managed to learn about the other occupants of the manor. Seeing as it's not much....'

'Go ahead.'

'First of all, Mademoiselle Féral will confirm my own testimony, because she never left my side. I don't think she'll be able to tell you any interesting new information. Madame de Malèves and her lady's maid, whose room was not far from the victim's, do not seem to have noticed much. The young servant thought she heard a detonation, but didn't attach much importance to it. That leaves my three friends in the lodge. They don't know anything.'

'Well,' concluded Machaux, 'it all seems rather obscure. Before I leave, I must definitely clear up the discrepancy between the valet and the cook regarding the detonation. It's the only "thread" we have for the moment. Would you be good enough to find the aforementioned Félix?'

'Of course.'

'Thank you.'

Two minutes later, Darlay returned in the company of the old servant.

'Sit down, my friend,' said the commissaire, consulting his notes. 'Would you go over, in detail, your actions after you finished the table settings in the dining room?'

'My actions?'

'Yes... everything you did from that moment on.'

Félix thought for a few seconds:

'Well, as I told you, Monsieur, I went upstairs to get a clean apron from the linen room. And whilst I was passing—.'

'Are you sure?... Maybe you went up the first time to find an apron... which you didn't take, but went downstairs and then up again a second time. It was only then that Monsieur Darlay and Mademoiselle Féral saw you in front of the door of Monsieur Antoine de Malèves' room.'

'Oh, no, Monsieur!'

'And you didn't hear a detonation?'

'No, Monsieur.'

'When you left the dining room, didn't you go to the kitchen?'

'Ah, yes. It's true, I did talk to Estelle for a minute or two.'

'And it was only afterwards that you went upstairs?'

'Yes, Monsieur.'

Commissaire Machaux seemed to pause for thought, then turned to the journalist.

'That was the same moment that you heard the detonation, I believe?'

'Yes, we arrived at the terrace.'

'Monsieur Darlay, could I ask you to fetch the cook?'

'But of course.'

Whilst the journalist was away, Machaux said nothing, contenting himself with giving Félix suspicious looks. Darlay brought in the fat Estelle.

'What is it now?' she asked rudely.

'Nothing... Just a clarification. It was after Félix left that you heard what sounded like a detonation, wasn't it?'

'No, you haven't understood a word. On the contrary, it was just before he arrived!'

'Are you sure?'

'That's what I said.'

Machaux seemed taken aback. He turned to Darlay.

'Are you sure you heard the detonation just as you reached the terrace?'

'Absolutely.'

The policeman appeared to give up. He dismissed Félix and Estelle, seemingly with regret.

'Really,' he said to the journalist, 'there's something incomprehensible going on... And not just regarding this matter, unfortunately.'

Dublard passed by the window of the smoking room.

'There's our novelist,' said Darlay. 'Would you like to see him?'

'Not at this moment, if you don't mind. I'd like to get my notes in order first. Go and chat with him. I'll join you when I've finished.'

Darlay went to find Dublard and bring him up to speed about Félix and Estelle and the detonation. They were coming into the corridor when Machaux joined them.

VI

Too many possible murderers

'Monsieur le commissaire,' said the reporter with emphasis, 'may I present my friend, Jules Dublard....'

Dublard inclined his pudgy figure.

'An author of detective fiction,' insisted the journalist slyly.

'Ah!' exclaimed Machaux. 'This manor is a hotbed of culture! I'd like your advice, Monsieur Dublard, because this business is beginning to resemble a detective novel.'

'Um...,' said Dublard, scurrying along behind Machaux, who was heading towards the staircase, 'you're joking, Monsieur le commissaire. I mean, our little stories... Although I must say, this murder doesn't surprise me one little bit.'

Machaux stopped.

'Well, well,' he said. 'And why is that?'

'Um..., that's to say, I mean... this story of a barricaded room where a crime is nevertheless committed... Classic situation... Cartesian drama of sorts. I've had a manuscript on my desk for several weeks about a similar case. I thought of calling it *Death out of Nowhere....*'

'Not bad,' said Machaux, who had started upwards again, 'but death, fortunately, always comes from somewhere.'

'Naturally, Monsieur le commissaire, but it's just for the title, to lure the reader... For us, fabricators of puzzles, explaining that sort of thing is as easy as ABC.'

Machaux, who had reached the landing, whistled in admiration, without turning around.

'My word!' he exclaimed. 'You certainly don't pull any punches. What am I doing here?'

'That's what I ask myself,' retorted Dublard rashly.

The remark took the policeman's breath away.

'Well I never!' he said indignantly.

Darlay intervened.

'Don't get upset. Dublard didn't mean to say he found your

41

presence uncalled for. Far from it.'

'Far from it,' agreed the novelist.

The journalist turned on his friend.

'Listen. Leave us alone. We'll—.'

'Yes,' interrupted Machaux disdainfully. 'You can provide your little explanations when we interrogate you.'

'All right,' replied Dublard in a conciliatory tone, 'What I was trying to say was....'

***

At the foot of the stairs, Le Bellec was waiting anxiously for Dublard.

'What did he say to you?'

'He didn't even question me. I tried to tell him my opinion, but you know, all those policemen are the same. I'm right to describe them in my books as not very bright and not very polite. Just you wait for my next commissaire, I'll ridicule him!'

'Don't work yourself into such a state,' advised Le Bellec. 'Come and make a tour of the park, that will do you good—and me too, as I don't feel very well.'

'What's wrong?'

'I feel sick in the stomach... This business, you know....'

'That's what I tried to explain to that policeman. I told him about my next book, *Death out of Nowhere*. Do you know what that imbecile replied? "Fortunately, it always comes from somewhere." I told him "naturally," but....'

The two friends were now walking past a row of dwarf rosebushes as they continued their tour of the manor.

'Ah, Dublard,' moaned Le Bellec, 'it's frightening.'

'Not at all! There's an easy explanation. These machinations about doors locked on the inside... my lawyer, for example....'

'It's not about that,' said Le Bellec, collapsing onto a bench. 'I don't give a damn about your lawyer. I'm thinking about Beaurieux.'

'What, still?'

'I can't help it... it's about the Emperor of China's coup. I had nightmares about it last night.'

Dublard gave his companion a look full of pity.

'Listen, Le Bellec, don't start that again. I've explained three times what happened.'

'You can say whatever you like. I'm frightened. He predicted everything... the exact time... the place... the circumstances....'

And Le Bellec, eyes bulging and full of nervous tics, stared fixedly at the closed window, behind which... Dublard, meanwhile, took a notebook out of his pocket and produced a pencil.

'I can see,' he said, 'that I haven't been sufficiently clear. So I'll try another method.'

'You should just let me talk to Darlay....'

'Wait a moment. He'll just laugh in your face and treat you like an imbecile, whilst I'm trying desperately to have a different opinion of you. For heaven's sake, just think for three minutes. Try to follow me.'

Dublard wrote in his notebook:

1. Motives for Beaurieux to murder Antoine de Malèves

Answer: to annoy Dublard.

'No, of course not,' said Le Bellec, who was reading over his friend's shoulder.

'Okay. Find another reason. He wanted to be his heir? They had the same mistress? Beaurieux had sworn, by the bedside of his dying mother, to kill a seventy-year-old butterfly collector?'

'Don't be an idiot,' replied Le Bellec with a faint smile.

'Consequently, my response is the correct one, and the only one. Beaurieux murdered Antoine de Malèves, for the sole purpose of putting my aptitude for detection to the test—just as he announced. It follows that:

a -,Beaurieux is mad

b - Beaurieux is a bloodthirsty brute.

'Choose between those two propositions... Ah! You see, you can't! Because you know very well that Beaurieux is the gentlest of men! A prankster, certainly, but one who wouldn't hurt a fly. As for being mad, we would have noticed, wouldn't we? And, in any case, a madman couldn't have perpetrated such a magnificent murder.

'Now, having reviewed the psychological impossibilities, let's examine the material ones and write:

2. Could Beaurieux have actually murdered Antoine de Malèves? Here, we don't need to think for a long time: the absurdity and

foolishness of the means used, the disproportion between a pirouette and a crime, the indisputable distance... I blush to be forced, because of your stubbornness, to state the obvious.

'There are incontestable facts: the movement, the light, the pusillanimity... Nonetheless, I have to see it through to the bitter end: Beaurieux, with the sheer magnetism of his look, hypnotised the fat Estelle and gave her the order to kill Uncle Antoine at the appointed hour... However, to impress us, he played his card trick. What do you think of that? You're right, there's no magnetism in Beaurieux's look, and hypnotism isn't capable of producing such an amazing feat, except in comic books.

'And so we arrive at the inevitable conclusion, obvious from the start: Beaurieux didn't murder Antoine de Malèves.

'That brings me to my third point:

3. How to explain Beaurieux's behaviour before the crime?

'There's only one logical, reasonable explanation. I'll tell you it for the third time. Beaurieux has a sensitive nature and is a very nervous type... Far from being a hypnotist, he would be, I think, a very good subject. And, although we may contest whether willpower can be strong enough to influence another person over time and distance, we do know, on the contrary, the undeniable facts of telepathy and divination... Our friend had been put in a particularly receptive state by our discussion about a fictitious crime, and it just so happened that, at that exact time, a real crime was taking place.

'Beaurieux had "sensed" that crime and interpreted his subconscious impressions in his usual manner, that is to say treating everything as a joke. What he really sensed was the actual time of the murder and a rough idea of the circumstances. The rest was just jiggery pokery. And the proof is his very real astonishment when he learnt what had happened.'

'Obviously... obviously,' repeated Le Bellec with a sigh.

***

Dublard, very pleased with himself, stretched his arms out on the back of the bench. He had a docile audience, and had no intention of stopping when things were going so well.

'Let's proceed further,' he continued. 'No, stay there, Le Bellec, I

44

was speaking figuratively. Now that we've established Beaurieux's innocence for certain, we ourselves can achieve the same result by applying *reductio ad absurdum* to prove that only he can be innocent: only he, or very nearly, that's to say, we two as well. That proof, naturally, is only valid for us, for someone not in our group could argue our triple complicity... Nothing would prevent us from hatching dark plans.'

'Please, Dublard, let's just accept we're not criminals. This is all wearing me down. But how could you think that any of our other friends...'

'Please, my little friend, I repeat that this drama is Cartesian. I wanted in vain to explain that to our poor superintendent. Do you imagine that this tale of closed shutters and locked doors can stop me? Would you like me to explain in detail how Pierre de Malèves went about killing his uncle?'

'Dublard, that's not possible!' exclaimed Le Bellec. 'Our friend... a criminal....'

'You're unbearable! I didn't say it was him! I believe the opposite, but I'm making deductions, exercising my mind... Let me talk, for heaven's sake! Good. Then here we go: Pierre has decided to do away with his uncle, for the inheritance ... or whatever... Fine. He comes back from his tour of the estate, just as he stated, and at the moment he reaches the north wing, he sees from the outside Antoine de Malèves coming out of the library... Are you following?'

'Yes, keep going.'

'He lets the old man go up the stairs, follows him on tiptoe and waits until his uncle has gone along the corridor and is ready to enter his room. At that moment, he fires... Antoine de Malèves, realising that he's been hit, throws himself into his room and instinctively locks the door with his key, before staggering a few steps and collapsing... Meanwhile, Pierre gets rid of the revolver in some hiding-place and waits. When the time comes, he'll appear from afar... What objections do you have to that theory?'

Le Bellec squeezed his arms against his chest in a sign of impotence. Dublard continued pitilessly:

'Let's leave Pierre with his simple little procedure. It's the kind of murder that wouldn't be in any of my books: no interest... How much more clever was the technique that Félix used!'

'What?' moaned Le Bellec. 'Was it really Félix?'

'Will you be quiet! I can see very well Félix waiting for Antoine de Malèves to return before closing the shutters. Once inside, he goes over to the window and opens it, but pretends that one of the shutters is jammed: he announces he's going to get a hammer and will be back in a minute, and leaves... Needless to say Uncle Antoine, who's at his writing desk, isn't going to go to the trouble of locking the door. That's what Félix is counting on. He takes his weapon, leaves the manor, goes to the rear and climbs the lime tree that faces the victim's window, about twenty metres away. Of course, everything has been checked out in advance. He shoots the old man in the back and sees him collapse; he calmly climbs back down, returns to the room, closes the shutters and the window, switches on the electricity, and leaves. One minute later, he will return and pretend to hear moans from inside the room....'

'Let me stop you right there,' said Le Bellec, getting excited despite himself. 'The door isn't locked from the inside.'

'But that's the clever part about it,' retorted Dublard, with a superior air. 'Félix arrives first... he gets hold of the door latch, pretends to shake it, and announces that the door is locked... Why would the others not believe him? They know it normally is. Straight away they try to break the door down. Once it's open, Félix just has to wait for the general confusion, surreptitiously turn the key, and the deception is complete.

'Now do you begin to understand why doors said to be locked aren't always? But that's not all. Allow me to reveal now how Darlay, using a completely different method, snuffed old de Malèves' life out.'

'Darlay now?' blubbered Le Bellec.

'He, of necessity, had to have an accomplice: Mademoiselle Féral. They'll get married afterwards, I assume. I must admit what he did was quite audacious. He first goes up to the empty attic room which is directly above the old man's room and hangs a length of rope down. Next, he goes down to the victim's room and knocks on the door. Antoine de Malèves opens it, then, as he turns his back to return to his desk, Darlay dispatches a bullet which sends him to join his ancestors.'

'That's horrible.'

46

'He turns the key in the lock, gently opens the window and the shutters, makes sure nobody is watching, and climbs out onto the sill. In passing, let me point out that the window is closed by a handle which slides a bar across. Consequently, as you pull the two halves of the window towards you from the outside, you can create the impression that the window is closed. Hanging from the rope, Darlay pushes the iron shutters towards each other, then, agile as he is, he climbs back into the attic and pulls up the rope. It's easy for him to descend to the park, avoiding the comings and goings of Félix, and get back with Mademoiselle Féral just before the valet sees them together.

'Let me remind you that Darlay claimed to have heard the shot at that time, but he must have been in form, because Félix himself heard nothing... When Darlay entered the room with the others, it was easy for him to go over to the window and, under the pretext of demonstrating that everything was shut, make sure that it was. Who would contradict him? Are you convinced?'

'Enough, Dublard,' whispered Le Bellec.

'But Darlay's cleverness doesn't mean I underestimate the horrible *sang-froid* of Hélène de Malèves, who profited from what her lady's maid... Hey, Le Bellec, what's the matter?'

But Le Bellec, blocking his ears and with his eyes popping out of his head, was running away across the park.

***

'Very good!' said Dublard to himself, very calmly.

He got up from the bench and stretched. The sun was high in the sky. He felt hungry all of a sudden, and the kitchen was close by. He tiptoed to the half-open window and raised himself up.

'Will we be eating soon, Estelle?'

'In a quarter of an hour or so, Monsieur Dublard.'

A quarter of an hour... the time to make another small trip. He was moving away, head down, with his gaze wandering over the cobblestones, when...

'Well, well, well,' he said, bending down.

His hand clutched an object gleaming feebly in the sun. He looked up. A few metres above him was the window of the crime room! The object had been well hidden under a tuft of grass between two stones.

'Could it by chance...' he thought.

He walked across the park, mulling over his discovery. Little by little his expression brightened, and he stopped suddenly with a gesture of triumph.

'Aha!' he said jubilantly, 'so, Monsieur le commissaire, you wanted to mock old Dublard. Well, you're not ready to learn what he's just worked out. From this moment, and for as long as I choose to remain silent, you'll have to resign yourself to this: there are indeed cases where death comes out of nowhere....'

VII

Insoluble problem

Whilst Dublard was constructing extravagant hypotheses, the commissaire, accompanied by the laboratory assistant and the journalist, had gone to M. Antoine de Malèves' room.

'If we could establish how the crime was committed,' said Machaux, 'we would be well on our way to finding the culprit.'

The policeman moved around the room with great care. Darlay, leaning against the door, watched him. Nothing had been moved, other than the corpse. There was no blood on the carpet.

The room was plainly furnished: a small bed , a wardrobe, a desk, two chairs and two armchairs. Everything was tidy, clean and in perfect order. Machaux examined the door very carefully. The key was in the lock, on the inside; the bolt was drawn. On the jamb, the strike plate, partly ripped out, barely held.

'The poor devil was definitely locked in,' said the policeman.

He went over to the window and opened it. He checked the iron shutters.

'You did take fingerprints, I assume,' he asked the specialist from the police technical laboratory.

'Yes, Monsieur le commissaire, but they were quite blurred. At first sight, they appear to be those of the victim.'

'That's what I thought. Besides,' he added, addressing Darlay, 'I only had them checked out of a sense of duty. I'm convinced the murderer didn't come in.'

He opened the shutters. Sunlight streamed in, dimming the effect of the electric lamp.

'Turn it off, please,' he said to the assistant.

He began to search the room inch by inch. For more than an hour he carefully examined the furniture and the carpet, without finding anything unusual. He went back to the door again, and then the window. The walls themselves did not escape his attention.

'It's fantastic,' he said, sitting down at the desk. 'There's nothing,

nothing....'

On the desk it was possible to discern a stamp catalogue buried under the disorderly stack of paper.

'Did Monsieur de Malèves own an impressive collection?' asked the policeman.

'Not that I know of. I don't think he was interested until recently.'

Machaux got up and made a face.

'Let's accept the médecin légiste's conclusion,' he said. 'The bullet was not fired in this room; the weapon was at least twenty metres away. We can't even be sure it was fired from the south wing. The only window it's possible to see from here isn't even ten metres away and is hardly set back at all. Who's staying there?'

'Beaurieux.'

'It's possible that an ancient weapon was used and the speed of the bullet was below average. And the médecin légiste could have made an error about the distance.'

He fell silent for a moment. Then he continued:

'The tower is completely masked by the wing. And notice as well that Madame de Malèves could not have been hit in the kidney by someone firing from the tower. For that, the victim would have to be sitting on the window sill... Is that likely?'

'Certainly not in Monsieur Antoine's case,' affirmed Darlay.

The commissaire, at the window, continued to examine the surroundings.

'Well, how about the lime trees?... It doesn't seem impossible for a good marksman... I'll take a look down there later on. Could you do something for me?'

'Please, just ask.'

'Would you go down to the kitchen? I'm going to manoeuvre the shutters; I'd like to find out what noise it will make.'

'Very well. I'll let you know.'

Shortly after, Darlay was back.

'I heard it clearly enough,' he said, 'but I think I should point out that for Estelle, it's such a familiar sound that she scarcely notices it. Plus which, she was mincing the meat.'

'You're right. Also, why would the old man have reopened the shutters that Félix had just closed half-an-hour before? And why, above all, would he have closed them after being shot?'

'It's not physically impossible,' observed Darlay, 'because he survived for almost forty-five seconds.'

'Certainly, but the action itself doesn't make sense. I concede, if I absolutely must, that if the attack had come from the corridor, the instinctive action would have been to throw himself against the door and lock it; but if it had come from the window, I completely fail to understand why the old man, shot in the kidney, would immediately realise the attack had come from outside and would carefully close the shutters and the window. That would mean him exposing himself, for several seconds more, to a second attack. To my mind, the only sensible act would be for him scramble out of reach in one corner of the room and shout for help, if he had the force.'

'He could have seen his assailant running away, in which case there would have been no danger of a new attack.'

'But that wouldn't explain why he closed the shutters! It doesn't make any sense. The sensible thing to do would have been to use his last remaining forces to try to open the door and call for help.'

'Everything you say is very true, obviously.'

'However,' continued Machaux, 'if the attack had come from the corridor, it seems impossible that the detonation wasn't heard very clearly by Madame de Malèves and her lady's maid, or even by Félix, on the floor below .'

They continued for a while, constructing hypotheses, but, one by one, they failed, faced with one impossibility or another. Finally, Machaux made a gesture of disappointment.

'We're going a round in circles,' he growled. 'I don't think we'll find out any more by staying in this damned room. I'm going to go through the papers I found in the desk and the wardrobe, carefully and with a clear head. This afternoon I'll look around the estate, then I'll go back to Versailles to see the juge d'instruction.'

He let his eyes wander around the room for the last time, pausing once to take in the high foliage of the lime trees.

'I don't mind telling you,' he said, 'that this is the most difficult case of my career. There are nothing but physical impossibilities, no matter which way you turn.'

'It's true,' acknowledged Darlay, 'that there hasn't been the slightest glimpse of clarity.'

'And yet,' said the policeman, irritably, 'a solution must exist!'

51

He gathered the papers he wanted to examine, and placed them in his black briefcase. Once he had finished, he turned to the journalist:

'Once I'm out of here, I might be able to think more clearly. Could I ask you, whilst I'm away, to make a note of anything you think might be useful for the investigation?'

'You can count on me,' said Darlay.

They left the room. In the corridor stood a gendarme, yawning.

'I don't need you any more, Legaret,' said the commissaire. 'You and your colleague may leave.'

At the foot of the stairs, Pierre de Malèves approached Darlay.

'I say, are we going to be able to pay our last respects?'

'Not yet, old man. The juge d'instruction has to authorise it. For the time being, the body has to stay in the tower.'

'Fair enough... Monsieur le commissaire, would you do us the honour of lunching with us?'

Machaux thanked him... Not enough time... He would make do with a sandwich.

'Good riddance,' muttered Dublard who, in the company of Beaurieux, was spying on him from a distance. 'He's ruined my appetite.'

VIII

Second inexplicable murder

The least one can say is that lunch was lacklustre. Mme. de Malèves, still suffering, did not come down and the lord of the manor, visibly preoccupied, cut his meal short, excusing himself to return to his wife before going about his regular business. Jeanne Féral, still shaken by recent events, ate half-heartedly and spoke in a soft voice. Le Bellec only lifted his nose out of his plate to roll his eyes anxiously. Darlay absent-mindedly rolled his bread into little balls. Only Dublard, philosophically, made a point of eating heartily. Beaurieux seemed excited, his gestures more animated and his look more brilliant than normal, as if he'd partaken of some form of alcoholic stimulant during the morning.

The atmosphere was oppressive, but no one wanted to raise the subject occupying all their thoughts; the phrases exchanged were insipid and rare.

As soon as the baron left, Beaurieux got up in turn, announcing that he had a headache. He was, he claimed, going to sleep "for an hour or two". Mister Buck, who had been going from one guest to another in the hunt for tasty morsels, installed himself peacefully in an empty chair. Outside, a storm was already brewing.

'Go on,' growled Dublard, giving Le Bellec a disdainful look. 'Get it off your chest, say something. He's gone....'

'I'll talk if I feel like it,' muttered Le Bellec. 'Unless I pack my suitcase and take the five o'clock train.'

'You'll talk to my face,' retorted Dublard. 'I'm not having you tell stories behind my back, do you understand, my lad?'

Le Bellec banged the table with his fist.

'Very well, I'll talk, but not here.' He shot a glance in Félix's direction. 'Let's go to the smoking room.'

'Would I be one too many?' asked Jeanne Féral.

'You, Mademoiselle? Not at all,' giggled Dublard. 'Nobody is too many to listen to the ramblings of Monsieur Le Bellec, even though his speech is addressed to Darlay most of all... Come along, Mademoiselle, the more publicity the better, the absurdity increases proportional to the number of listeners.'

'I don't understand anything about your precautions,' interceded Darlay. 'Le Bellec has something to say. Let's proceed to the smoking room.'

***

As soon as they were all seated in the smoking room, separated by a simple door from the dining room, Le Bellec turned to the novelist:

'Go ahead, Dublard, speak,' he sighed.

'That's too much! You're the one who opens the can of worms and now you're the one who wants to get out of it.'

'That's it? Should I leave?' grumbled Darlay.

Le Bellec was like a man throwing himself into the water.

'Oh, very well,' he mumbled. 'Dublard can mock me all he likes, but I can tell you that he, Beaurieux and I were warned that a crime would take place at the manor.'

'What did you say?' said Darlay slowly.

And he sat there with his mouth open, in an expression of utter stupefaction. Jeanne Féral, frozen in her armchair, squealed and put her hands to her lovely face, her eyes wide open.

'There, there,' said Dublard paternally. 'I was sure you'd start by saying something stupid. Don't get alarmed, Lucien, I'll tell you the facts. I prefer to do the talking myself, because it has to be said. You've heard of the peculiar phenomenon known as telepathy, I assume?'

'Of course.'

'Well, this famous story of Le Bellec's can be summarised as follows: yesterday, a few moments before the incident, Beaurieux, who never left our sight for the whole afternoon, had a sort of prophetic crisis. He suddenly announced that he was capable of killing on command and challenged me to prove his guilt. You will readily grasp that, sensitive as he is, he was interpreting in his own way some vague premonition, which he proceeded to treat as a joke.'

'But,' objected Le Bellec feebly, 'it was you, Dublard, who chose the time of the crime— .'

'Much ado about nothing,' cut in the journalist. 'You're both completely crazy!'

'I repeat,' continued Dublard, ignoring Darlay's vexing interruption, 'that if, as you say, I chose the time of the crime, it was by pure coincidence; I didn't want to keep the joke going until the following day. But if it had, you can be sure that the crime would have been committed all the same. I'll let you be the judge, Lucien. Just look how the loopy operation of Beaurieux's took place... For, anticipating Le Bellec's little scheme, I took the precaution of bringing a pack of cards.'

'A pack of cards?' murmured Darlay, incredulous.

'Of course, because Le Bellec isn't sure whether a murder can be committed with a pack of cards... Wait, I also need a red mat and a handkerchief knotted in all four corners.'

'Ah, ah!' exclaimed the journalist, seized by an unseemly impulse to laugh.

The fat Dublard, with his strange bonnet, presented an irresistibly droll figure. Jeanne Féral, too, had difficulty keeping a straight face.

'Watch carefully,' said Dublard, 'you too, miss. Watch how one goes about giving registration clerks nightmares... One takes the king of spades..., the ace of diamonds..., the ace of hearts..., one places them on the red mat... and one throws the king of spades on the floor, shouting:

'*And the Emperor of China be damned!*'

'It's completely idiotic,' concluded Darlay.

There was a knock on the door; Félix appeared, bringing coffee.

'Messieurs are playing Patience?' he observed stiffly.

'No, Félix, we're conducting an experiment. Please close the door.'

'Excuse me, I believe the baron is here.'

Pierre de Malèves came into the smoking room.

'How's Hélène?' asked Jeanne Féral.

'Better, thank you, I hope she'll be able to dine with us tonight. A cup of coffee would be most welcome.'

'Very well,' said Dublard. 'I'm sure Miss Féral will oblige.'

The sentence ended in tumult. Everyone sat up. Le Bellec screamed.

Very clearly, the sound of a nearby shot that had just been fired came through the still-open door.

'Hélène! Hélène!' cried Pierre de Malèves.

He bounded up the stairs, followed by all the others; on the upper landing he shouted for joy: Mme. de Malèves was waiting anxiously in the doorway of her room. Beautiful, heavy locks framed her irregular but gracious features.

'I heard a detonation,' she said anxiously, burying herself against her husband's shoulder.

The others jostled in the corridor.

'It's nothing, because you're here.'

'Where's Léontine?' asked Darlay.

'I sent her out to gather some roses for me.'

The journalist went into her room and over to the window, where he could see the lady's maid running towards the park railings.

'Estelle went into the village,' observed the lord of the manor.

'And Beaurieux?' stammered Le Bellec.

It was true. That only left....

'He announced that he was going to take a siesta in his room,' someone said.

Hadn't he heard the shot? Darlay almost ran to the adjacent wing, to his friend's door.

'Beaurieux,' he called out.

Nothing moved. The door was locked and, looking through the keyhole, Darlay immediately saw it was locked from inside.

'Ah!' sobbed Le Bellec. 'He's killed himself!'

'Imbecile!' growled Dublard.

Just as the day before, shoulders had to be applied to the door: a panel cracked. Through the opening, the journalist was able to glimpse....

'Pierre,' he said in an expressionless voice, 'take the ladies away... Go away, Le Bellec. Dublard and Félix, help me.'

The door was flung wide open.

***

'He's dead,' said Dublard, running a hand around his collar, as if he were strangling himself. Darlay, kneeling, patted the inert body.

'How... but how...,' he repeated dully. 'Ah! My god, here.'

He indicated a hole at the base of the cranium.

The corpse lay collapsed upon itself, near a closed interior door: the half-open eyes seemed to be pursuing a dream; the features were calm. Death must have been very sudden.

'A bullet in the cerebellum,' Darlay noted mechanically.

He looked around for the weapon. In vain. He went over to the window and shook it. It was well and truly closed, and the panes were intact.

A moaning noise came from the corridor. Near the broken door, Le Bellec, looking like a madman, pointed a finger at the dead man:

'See,' he groaned... 'the Emperor of China's coup... Death out of nowhere!...'

IX

A new way to kill oneself?

'We have to call the police at once,' said the journalist.

'But, Monsieur, that's impossible,' murmured the valet, who was trembling. 'The telephone doesn't work on Sundays.'

'That's true, it's Sunday. It has to be done from the village. Send Gourvet on his bicycle. The telephone cabin is in the grocery store. He needs to call the gendarmerie at Mantes and alert Superintendent Machaux.'

Dublard had led Le Bellec away in the company of the ladies, and Pierre de Malèves had returned to join Darlay. There were tears in his eyes.

'It's horrible, Lucien... Poor Louis....'

'There's no doubt he was murdered,' said the journalist sadly.

Standing in the middle of the room, he was swaying as if he were drunk. A cold shiver ran up his spine and he felt his shirt sticking to his shoulders. Unable to speak, he drew on his willpower. He could still move and act, even if only mechanically. Only with action would he regain control of himself.

He made his way carefully around Beaurieux's corpse and opened the interior door that it was blocking. Behind it, he knew, was a half-bathroom. Everything was in its normal state of semi-disorder; nothing suspicious. The "bull's-eye" (1) which provided light to the small room was closed. Discouraged, he closed the door. The mystery was crushing him. Nevertheless, before going back to the middle of the room, he forced himself to look at the corpse he had to by-pass and noticed something protruding slightly... a notebook. He pulled it out gently, rejoined de Malèves, and opened it.

He couldn't read it.

'Let's go outside,' he said, pushing his friend.

The valet reappeared.

---

(1) a circular transom on a horizontal axis, common in old French houses

'It's done, Monsieur. Gouvret has gone.'

Darlay, for better or for worse, closed the damaged door.

'Stay close to the stairs, would you, Félix? I don't want anybody in the wing.'

'Very well, Monsieur... Has Monsieur visited the other rooms in the wing?'

'No, but I shall do so in order to reassure you.'

In addition to Beaurieux's room and the half-bathroom, there was, on the opposite side of the corridor, the apartment reserved for Jeanne Féral, comprising a room and a boudoir. The journalist checked it rapidly.

'Rest assured, Félix,' he said. 'There's no one here in this part of the manor, which isn't very large. Besides, we're not leaving.'

'Very well, Monsieur, I shall sit on the first step of the staircase. Monsieur will understand that my legs are rather weak.'

'Pierre,' asked the reporter, 'could you take everyone downstairs or into the park? I'm going to my room for a moment. The police won't be here for another hour.'

'Don't you want to search the grounds?'

'I don't think that would be useful.'

Once in his room, Darlay slumped down in an armchair and had a moment of weakness. He had known Beaurieux for such a long time. That death....

Then he went to the sink, bathed his face and, returning to his armchair somewhat calmed, opened the notebook. The more he read, the more horror and stupefaction invaded his soul.

***

"It would be unworthy to order a death with such a stupid phrase."

It was clearly Beaurieux's writing, the notes scribbled in pencil, with no concern for order or neatness. Sometimes a single phrase occupied a whole page, with large, jagged letters; elsewhere, the words seemed to chase each other across the page. There was a bit of everything: addresses, shopping notes, quotations from poets and philosophers (with the author's name in parentheses) ; and then, here and there, amidst the jumble, phrases which would catch the eye, such as the one Darlay saw when he first opened the notebook.

As he garnered phrases here and there, a terrible sense of unease came over him:

"...How many men, through the ages, have found a truly original method of causing death?"

"Obviously, never write anything down which could explain how... It's all right for me to read, but if someone else should and be unable to resist the temptation, what a responsibility! What impunity!"

"One could also say: a machine for creating an alibi."

"And the Emperor of China, etc... it could take months to modify that phrase."

"... Try not to put the funnel on the head... start with a handkerchief, then, little by little, nothing."

"...Really, it works with a blue mat, but better not make even a small change."

"That strange phrase attracts too much attention. But replacing it by a banality (example: it will rain tomorrow) creates the danger it could be pronounced by anyone and set everything off by mistake."

"...What a laugh to see Dublard's face."

"... it's quite simply an awakening, and it's marvellous to see."

"... The king of spades could be replaced by the king of clubs or the queen of spades: what's important is to have a black figure between two red aces."

"...The best: operate without witnesses, but in such a way that the presence was undeniable... in a place where impossible to communicate with anyone without being seen by witnesses. Thus alibi assured, without having attracted attention."

"...Like a conjuring trick, in other words. The simpler it is, the less one thinks about it."

***

'My God!' thought Darlay. 'Why didn't I think of it before? Was it a detective story plot that Beaurieux was constructing to propose to Dublard, or was he planning to write it himself?'

Yes, but Beaurieux was dead within a minute of Dublard's demonstration, just as Antoine de Malèves was dead within a minute of Beaurieux's.

The journalist, his head in his hands, felt he was losing his reason as his thoughts whirled inside his cranium like a flock of startled birds.

Coincidences? Maybe... No, surely. And all the good reasons which Dublard had accumulated to convince Le Bellec, Darlay found to convince himself.

But even if there were coincidences, that didn't clear up the puzzle. What sense could be made of those two stupid murders with nothing resembling a motive to explain them? And just who could be the perpetrator? None of the residents of the manor could have physically executed them; none of the peasants in the region was capable of such an infernal ingenuity and, furthermore, no strange presence had been detected in the park or its surroundings in the last two days.

In any case, a murderer, even unknown, even vanished, can be sensed... they leave traces. In all the criminal cases the journalist had covered in the last few years, he always had the normal impression of a flesh-and-blood culprit. Here, not so... Death occurred, engendered by an act manifestly lacking any human intervention, as if by spontaneous generation.

Even so, a bullet which kills doesn't come out of thin air and through walls simply by incantation. If one could imagine that a magical operation could kill from afar, like for example, a terribly rapid bewitchment (if bewitchments exist), then death would arrive in the form of a simple cessation of life, an inhibition of the nervous system... The death itself would appear natural, even though it might be inexplicable. But there wouldn't be a wound from a weapon. Magical waves, magnetic or otherwise, don't use revolvers!

Therefore there must be a weapon somewhere, fired at close range or from afar by some unknown means. And, like it or not, the bare fact was that there was only one light in the darkness: Beaurieux's little notebook... Without it....

***

I haven't approached this properly, thought Darlay, whose brain was starting to become more lucid. I simply rejected Beaurieux's explanation out of hand. Why not go back and admit that, in defiance of all probability, the truth lies there? After all, when scientists pursue their theories, they often stumble upon unexpected consequences.

So, let's start by accepting that Beaurieux has discovered a truly original way to kill.

"...How many men, through the ages...."

Yes, and by what extraordinary combination of circumstances was this remarkable and terrible distinction accorded by Fate to this amiable fellow, intelligent enough, but lazy, superficial, and unambitious: happy to have a position as supervisor?

"...Like a conjuring trick, in other words. The simpler it is, the less one thinks about it."

That, in fact, is right up Beaurieux's street: childish as a young student, lover of noisy nightlife, sounder of alarms, singer of serenades to the moon.

Let's just accept it! He has found, purely by accident, something stupid... a strange farce. Of course, he couldn't do it twice to the same friend, or the other would have understood. One could also try it on Dublard.

"...What a laugh...."

Except, in someone else's hands, someone with evil intentions, the farce in question could become dangerous and even, as Beaurieux realised, an instrument of death. A strange, weird instrument which allowed all alibis. But the idea of actually using it to kill never even crossed the fantasist's mind, that was certain: he merely thought about mystifying his friend.

And that was what was so staggering. Unbeknown to Beaurieux, the terrible power latent in what he considered to be a joke was suddenly released, as if a child's firecracker had blown up the house. Thus it was that the machine so meticulously constructed functioned implacably. Beaurieux, the unfortunate sorcerer's apprentice, was powerless to rein in the forces unleashed, and even became a victim himself... He had delivered, not his secret, but the way to use it, and the frightful occult energy he had sparked killed him.

And it's Dublard who....

***

But then how, in Beaurieux's mind, was the farce he'd prepared for Dublard to take effect? Because something had to happen as a result.

Maybe an insignificant disaster... the death of a chicken... which was of little importance in the scheme of things, after all. What was weird was the total lack of proportion between the feeble means and the frightful result: two corpses in locked rooms.

'No! No!' Darlay berated himself, his hands clutching his hair. 'All that is grotesque and impossible! I'm getting senile.'

But a voice louder than reason murmured tenaciously: 'Admit it! Admit it!'

If the solution was as easy to find as Beaurieux believed, Darlay should be able to discover it as well. *"The simpler it is, the less one thinks about it."* And Dublard himself, who had twice been a witness...

Yes, but how to get Dublard to admit he had realised or suspected the truth? To do so, for the novelist, would be to recognise that he had been the agent of his friend's death which, deep down, he must desperately deny. If there was one person from now on who would refuse to give any credibility to "the Emperor of China's coup", it would have to be the unfortunate Dublard!

So therefore Darlay would have to find it for himself. But where to look? Nothing made sense, it was all shadows, gestures, phrases, a conjuring trick. The police would arrive soon. Firmly planted in reality, they would look at how the doors opened for the murderer, which hand had held the weapon. They would find fingerprints, traces, motives. Death doesn't ride on dreams!....

But the voice continued to murmur tenaciously, pitilessly: 'Admit it! Admit it!'

The police still hadn't arrived. Darlay left his room to go downstairs. Félix was still there, sitting on the stairs.

'Monsieur,' he demanded anxiously, 'do I have to stay here alone?'

'Come down with me,' said the journalist. 'You can stay in the middle of the corridor and watch both staircases.'

'Thank you, Monsieur. I would prefer that.'

Darlay pushed open the door of the smoking room: nobody there.

The salon was also empty.

He found everyone gathered in the library.

It was a vast room, always rather dark because heavy green curtains masked most of the windows and what light there was was absorbed by leather-bound books and deep armchairs.

As soon as the journalist appeared, all discussion ceased.

Pierre de Malèves got up and approached him.

'Lucien,' he said in a low voice, 'it's terrible... *There's a pack of cards missing....*'

X

No! No! Darlay!...

'Why is that terrible?' asked Darlay.

Le Bellec raised his voice:

'Because that pack of cards wasn't taken for no reason,' he said.

'We're at the mercy of whoever has hidden it,' added Jeanne Féral, her features haggard under her untidy hair.

'Look at what you've become,' said the journalist slowly.

'That's what I keep telling them,' exclaimed Dublard. 'They're all going off the rails. They're up to their necks in this cock-and-bull story. In the twentieth century! In a manor lacking all modern comforts. All of this is Le Bellec's fault!'

'Good grief!'

'Quite so. You get on our nerves with your whining voice. And you're forever complicating matters. You'd be better off trying to make people forget you. You're the one mainly responsible for Beaurieux's death.'

'You're mad,' protested Le Bellec.

'I know what I'm talking about. With the face you were pulling since yesterday evening, Beaurieux realised that you were going to cause trouble. I'm convinced that after lunch he stayed listening behind his door... I don't know what was going through the poor fellow's mind, but he believed he was under suspicion and... he killed himself, it's obvious!'

'Where's the weapon?' interceded Pierre de Malèves.

'Where's the murderer?' retorted Dublard. 'Have you all forgotten the elementary rules of common sense? Isn't it simpler to admit the disappearance of a revolver, which will be discovered sooner or later, than to believe in the murderous power of a pack of cards and a stupid, meaningless phrase?'

"I knew this would happen," thought Darlay. "Dublard will never let himself be convinced. But isn't he right, and aren't I just as crazy as the others?"

'So our uncle killed himself as well?' murmured Hélène de Malèves, pressed against her friend.

'That has nothing to do with it,' replied Dublard, 'but this is not the time or the place to say why.'

'How did you come to discover that a pack of cards was missing?' asked Darlay.

'It wasn't difficult,' replied the lord of the manor. 'There are two: one in the lodge—which is the one that has disappeared—and the other is here.'

'And the red mats?'

'They're both here. One was over in the roadhouse and we brought it here.'

'Well,' observed the journalist, 'if one pack of cards was taken but neither of the mats, there's nothing to indicate an aggressive intent on the part of the... whoever did it. On the contrary, it looks more like a precautionary measure. You all had the same reaction, because you brought over the second pack and the two red mats.'

'But, if that were the case,' observed Jeanne Féral, 'why didn't whoever did that come forward?'

'Perhaps he's dead,' suggested Le Bellec with a sigh.

'There you go,' raged Dublard, 'you're doing it again! Now you want to make us admit that Beaurieux feared a second catastrophe.'

'He wasn't wrong,' retorted the other.

'You're all acting like children,' stated Darlay. 'Do you trust me? Give me that pack of cards... and don't talk to me again about that stupid story.'

One by one they consented, grumbling. The journalist put the pack in his pocket.

'Do you want some good advice? Don't sit in here staring at each other. We're all unhappy enough without adding disputes.'

'You're right,' agreed Pierre de Malèves. 'Are you coming, little one?' he said to his wife. 'This room is too depressing.'

'Oh! I don't want to go back upstairs,' replied Hélène, shivering.

'Well, then, we'll go into the salon, where you can rest better. Are you coming with us, Jeanne?'

'Yes, I'd like to,' said the young woman.

'If it's like that,' declared Dublard, 'let's bestir ourselves as well. Shall we go for a walk, stubborn one?'

Le Bellec got up.

'I'll come with you,' said the reporter. 'The walk will do us good. Ho, Mister Buck. Are you coming as well, old dog?'

***

The three friends walked without talking across the undergrowth which extended behind the manor. Darlay had picked up a dead branch, which he tapped discreetly against the trunks of trees. Dublard, his hands behind his back, thought obscure thoughts and Le Bellec followed behind, twisting his head from side to side, as if expecting some form of menace. Mister Buck ran around them, happy about the promenade. Soon the buildings of the farm came into view.

'Let's go as far as there,' proposed Darlay.

The friends soon arrived in the yard, silent and deserted in the Sunday afternoon.

'If Pagnaud is there, we can ask him for a drink,' suggested Dublard. 'I'm thirsty.'

It was true that the fat fellow was sweating profusely, despite the mild temperature. The farmer, hearing footsteps, was waiting in his doorway, watching them approach with their haggard looks.

'So,' he said, 'these messieurs. What misfortune brings them here? Will you come inside for a moment?'

His wife was there, in the dimly lit kitchen, with her two children. Lying on the table was a hunting rifle and some cartridges.

'You're cleaning your rifle, Pagnaud?'

The man winked:

'I'm acting as if I was hunting boar, Monsieur Darlay. You have to watch your step these days... with what's happening.'

'Victor,' begged his wife, 'don't take any risks.'

'Me?' protested the farmer. 'That's not what I'm doing. I only want to say that if someone I don't like starts coming around, I'll speak to him. Meanwhile, we can talk more freely in front of a pot. So, sit you down.'

'Aren't your farm hands here?' asked Darlay.

'On a Sunday afternoon? What do you think?'

And, curious as much as anxious, he started to ask a hundred questions about what had happened, and lamented the situation, together with his wife. After a while, Darlay got up and, seemingly preoccupied, went outside to wander about in the yard. Dublard, meanwhile, was starting to regret his desire to quench his thirst, so annoying were these good folk with their incessant questions. Whilst he was replying with evasive answers, Le Bellec, looking up at the ceiling, had an inspiration:

'I say, Madame Pagnaud, would you happen to have a room available?'

When she replied in the affirmative, he begged her to rent him one for a few days, naming her own price.

'What's up with you?' asked Dublard, who was listening with one ear. 'Don't you want to stay in the manor any more?'

'Thanks, but I'm fed up with living there, with nightmares all through the night.'

They started to squabble, with highfalutin phrases which the farmers were unable to understand. Le Bellec dug his heels in and obtained a room which Pagnaud dared not refuse him. Dublard, shrugging his shoulders, nevertheless accompanied him when he asked to see the room in question.

'Good for you,' he grumbled. 'That's going to make Pierre happy. Really clever of you.'

'Don't worry, it's my business. And Pierre will understand very well. I'll get my suitcase.'

'Very well. I'll tell you later, man to man, what I think.'

'You can think what you like. I'll see you soon, messieurs-dame.'

'After all,' observed the fat novelist, 'It's stupid of me to get involved in your little schemes. Where's Darlay?'

The journalist wasn't in the yard, nor in the surrounding area. They weren't about to chase after him. No doubt, forgetting about his friends, he was off pursuing another illusory trail elsewhere.

'Instead of grousing,' suggested Le Bellec, 'you'd be better off doing as I do. There are two beds.'

'Don't count on it, my lad. We haven't the same character, you and I. I'm not going to be a deserter.'

Whilst they were walking, Dublard kept shooting pitying looks at the sad Le Bellec, cowardly and reticent, congratulating himself for being able to maintain friendship with such a characterless individual. They retraced their steps in silence. When the towering façade of

Breule manor appeared through the trees, Le Bellec started to tremble again.

'All right, come with me,' said Dublard paternally. 'You're right. I can see you're not cut out for high drama.'

'What a sinister building.'

'Come along, I'll help you. Imbecile, you're more dear to me now that I've lost a friend.'

Arm in arm, they supported one another tearfully, aiming for the small entrance in the north wing.

'Will you accompany me... upstairs?' murmured Le Bellec.

'Of course! Of course! But first let's see if there's anything new.'

Dublard went to the library and stuck his head in the door.

'Monsieur Dublard,' said a muffled voice.

He couldn't see anyone... He went in, with Le Bellec on his heels.

***

Jeanne Féral was there alone, slumped in an armchair.

'What's up?' asked Dublard anxiously. The frightened young woman tried to straighten up and raise herself... She stammered unintelligibly as she pointed towards one of the windows; she seemed about to faint.

'Please, I beg you,' said Dublard, 'say something.'

'Darlay,' she gasped at last. 'There... the lodge....'

'Well what? Darlay?'

She tried to pull herself together:

'Run,' she whispered. '*He's just taken a red mat.*'

Le Bellec was already jostling Dublard.

'Do you hear that? He's taken a red mat! He has the cards! He wants to study the trick by himself! We must run and stop him, Dublard! He'll kill us!'

Terrified, he was already through the corridor and running outside. He showed such agility that the fat Dublard gave up trying to run after him. Soon out of breath, he was happy to follow behind at his own pace.

'I don't know why I'm even going,' he said to himself. 'Damn! I'm stopping. There are crazy people amongst us, but who? Good grief, what now?'

71

He saw, above the flower beds, the little Le Bellec approaching the roadhouse, and heard him cry:

'No! No! Darlay! Wait, don't do it!'

But suddenly the journalist himself came out of the lodge and, disregarding Le Bellec, began to run as well, past the spindle trees and in the direction of the south wing.

All Dublard could see of him was his long upper body. Then he heard Le Bellec's desperate cry as he entered the lodge.

'That's it!' he told himself. 'Darlay has performed the Emperor of China's coup!'

An unexpected sensation of anguish and weakness came over him, and when the inevitable shot came, he let himself flop down on the grass.

XI

In the empty manor

Hélène de Malèves was lying, like a delicate broken flower, on the salon carpet.

'Hélène! My little Hélène,' sobbed Pierre de Malèves.

When the detonation had rung out, he had rushed like a madman into the room only a few metres away and, followed by Félix, had thrown himself towards his inanimate wife. Crying, he had held her in his arms and now, sitting on the floor, he clutched the inert, blood-streaked body against his chest. Félix, haggard, kneeling by his side, looked around the coldly elegant salon, where there was no trace of the impossible murderer.

Meanwhile, Darlay's silhouette appeared in the doorway and, after a brief pause, advanced like a sleepwalker and crouched down next to the young woman.

'Lucien,' moaned the lord of the manor, 'who is the scoundrel who did this?'

'We'll find out,' said the journalist in a lifeless voice. 'Pierre, all is not lost. She's alive.'

He quickly pulled out a knife and proceeded to slit the left sleeve of the corsage up to the neckline, to reveal the white flesh of the shoulder.

'Don't move, Pierre, whatever you do. Keep pressing her against you. Félix, go and get me cotton, a bandage, whatever you can find.'

'I'll go to the bathroom, Monsieur. There's a medicine cabinet there.'

'My God! She's dead!' blubbered de Malèves, sensing his wife's head roll against his.

'Not so. I'm telling you she's alive. The bullet lodged above the heart. We have to find a surgeon immediately.'

'But how? There's no telephone. The nearest surgeon is twenty kilometres away.'

'We have to do whatever we can. As soon as the arm has been

bandaged, you have to go and get the car. Take Hélène to Saint-Germain and have her operated on as quickly as possible. Stay calm, Pierre. You have to save your wife!'

'You're right, Lucien.'

A few moments later, Darlay had completed a rough bandage.

'Lay her down on the carpet, Pierre. Bring the car onto the terrace. Félix, stay there.'

Whilst the lord of the manor ran to the garage, the journalist tried to find help. He was afraid he would not find anyone. In the library, a slender form lay on the sofa... Jeanne Féral had fainted.

'Too bad,' he said to himself. 'She'll wake up soon... on to more urgent things.'

Dublard staggered in from the park.

'Go and help Mademoiselle Féral,' ordered Darlay, pushing him into the library without listening to his mumbling.

The journalist came back into the salon. The noise of the motor car could be heard outside. He leant over Mme. de Malèves and, with the greatest of care, took the slender body into his arms.

'Let me do it,' he said to Pierre, who had just come in.

He carried Hélène to the awaiting vehicle and the three men laid the still-unconscious woman on the rear banquette of the spacious interior.

'I'll sit beside her until we get to the farm,' said the journalist. 'Then Gourvet's wife or Léontine can take over. Drive, Pierre.'

The gendarmes arrived at the manor less than a quarter of an hour after the vehicle left. The entrance door was wide open. As no one replied to the sound of the bell, the brigadier ventured into the hall....

'There's nobody here!' he exclaimed.

His voice echoed strangely inside the vast residence. Air currents caused doors to shut. Manifestly, the manor was empty.

'Well I never,' murmured the brigadier.

He returned to the front door, left one of the gendarmes to guard it, and asked the other to follow him.

'We're going to take a look around,' he said. 'We'll see.'

Together they went into the salon to their left. It was empty, but on the carpet, almost in the centre, a brown stain attracted the brigadier's attention. He bent over.

74

'Oh, oh!' he said.

He went down on his knees and touched the thick liquid with his finger.

'But it's blood!' said the gendarme as he watched.

'Yes, blood... and still fresh.'

For a moment they were bewildered. There was no trace of disturbance in the room.

'Well I never!' said the brigadier again.

Then he continued:

'Let's get going... let's see what else we find.'

They went out through the door to the corridor. The library was empty. So were the billiard room, the smoking room and the dining room, which they visited next. They went into the kitchen quarters in the south wing.

'Anybody there?' the brigadier called out.

There was no reply. Everything had been abandoned, pots, pans, plates, etc....

They went upstairs. In the corridor of the south wing, the brigadier called out again, in vain. But then he noticed that the door of the last room on the left appeared to have been broken in:

'Let's take a look,' he said to the gendarme.

He gave a start as he pushed the door open. The body of Beaurieux blocked a corner of the room, near the window.

'What the...,' swore the chief as he approached it.

The rigidity of the corpse indicated that death had occurred several hours ago. There was a clear trace of a bullet wound on the neck.

'Maybe they're all dead,' said the gendarme nervously.

The brigadier didn't reply directly to that tragic hypothesis, but everything in his manner indicated that he didn't reject it.

'Luckily I notified the commissaire,' he said, as if to calm himself.

Then, with an obvious effort, he declared:

'We shall have to visit all the rest of the manor.'

The following inspection yielded nothing sensational, other than that most of the rooms were in serious disorder, as if their occupants had left hurriedly without taking anything with them. The two gendarmes went downstairs via the stairs in the north wing and joined the sentry on guard at the front entrance. The brigadier, who seemed overwhelmed by events, decided at first to await the arrival of commissaire Machaux. Then, after a quarter-of-an-hour of unnerving inactivity, he decided to visit the little lodge and make a reconnaissance of the woods.

'We have to see what we had to have seen,' he explained to his bemused associates.

They swooped down on the "roadhouse". Once out of the silent manor and revived by the fresh air, the three gendarmes recovered their equilibrium. The one who had visited the rooms with the brigadier expressed mild astonishment.

'From now until we find all the others slain in the "shack,"' he said, indicating the lodge, 'won't be long.'

The brigadier, who was marching slightly ahead, muttered a few unintelligible words. Nevertheless, it was with a certain apprehension that he pushed open the door of the little lodge. They went in. At first they glimpsed nothing out of the ordinary, but then one of them uttered a cry of surprise which startled the others.

In one corner of the room, a man was sitting on a pouffe... It was old Félix. He was shivering with fear. The brigadier called out to him brutally:

'What the devil are you doing there, you? Come over here so we can see you.'

In fact, they had to help the old valet get up, and even then he could hardly stand. His eyes were wide with fear and he stammered incoherently.

'The walls shoot... Monsieur Beaurieux after Monsieur Antoine, Madame... Haunted manor... Bang! Bang!... Death....'

The brigadier shook him roughly, which was hardly the best method to calm him down.

'What's this all about?' he shouted. 'What are you talking about? Where are the lord and lady of the manor and the guests?'

Félix made a vague gesture.

'The revolver kills all by itself,' he stammered. 'It's terrible.'

He withdrew into total silence, all his limbs trembling. Then, released by the gendarme, he sat down on the floor and attempted to reach his pouffe. The brigadier gave the order to take him back to the mansion. Whereupon Félix resisted with all his might, swearing that a phantom was killing everyone and that no one should set foot in that vast residence.

Out of desperation, the gendarmes left him at the door of the lodge. The three of them looked at one another, taken aback and indecisive.

'We have to wait for the commissaire,' said the brigadier, once more.

At that very moment, he heard the noise of an argument. Shouts were emanating from the copse which separated the lodge from the south wing of the manor.

'Let's look into this,' he said, dragging his two men along with him.

They had hardly reached the high foliage when they encountered Dublard and Mlle. Féral. The latter rushed towards them:

'With the Emperor of China's coup,' she said, in a panic. 'It's kill... kill....'

She had let herself fall to the brigadier's knees, which he found very embarrassing.

'Come, come,' he said.

Dublard cut in:

'Don't listen to her! She's crazy. They're all crazy, for that matter.'

'The Emperor of China...' the young woman repeated.

Dublard, beside himself, almost threw himself upon her to strangle her. One of the gendarmes blocked him. Finally, they all left the woods and walked towards the manor.

'Where are the others?' asked the brigadier.

'How should I know?' replied Dublard irritably. 'They're all nuts!'

A car arrived at high speed from the south drive, which encircled the French garden. Commissaire Machaux got out. The brigadier, Dublard, and Mlle. Féral all clamoured for his attention. It was his turn to be stunned, but he recovered rapidly, leaving the two gendarmes with the Dublard-Féral couple, and leading the brigadier into the smoking room. Five minutes later, the latter came out. He didn't look proud of himself.

'Monsieur le commissaire would like to see you,' he said, addressing himself to Jeanne Féral and the novelist.

Then, turning to the gendarmes:

'Go and get the old man from the lodge. If he doesn't want to walk, carry him.'

XII

The fourth death coup

'Well, there you are!' exclaimed Commissaire Machaux, seeing Darlay approach. 'I was beginning to give up!'

'I was scouring the area,' explained the journalist.

'I see. More likely you were scouring the countryside, like the others!'

'You're admitting then....'

'I understand. There's something in what you say. I've been sweating blood for more than two hours. Are you going to tell me the same tall stories as your companions?'

'I don't know what they've told you.'

Night was falling, and through the windows of the smoking room and beyond the French garden, the leaves could be seen turning the same soft mauve as the twilight. Machaux paced up and down, deep in thought, between the low armchairs.

'What's going on?' he said. 'I'm told the massacre continues, I race here, and the place is deserted. A body in one of the rooms, blood in the salon, gendarmes who don't know anything—or, rather, repeat shocking gossip gathered elsewhere: it appears that people die here by magic, helped along by cabalistic formulas... No, let me speak! We end up dragging the valet out of who-knows-what hole; with eyes as wide as saucers, he declares that the mansion is haunted and that shots fire themselves. He doesn't know anything else. They bring in your friend Dublard—yes, the detective fiction writer—with the girl who was wandering in the woods. There's no way to get any sense out of her: she babbles about the Emperor of China and Dublard shuts her up, saying she's crazy. He is too, by the way. As for Le Bellec, he's quite simply disappeared. And you, what are you going to tell me about? The king of spades... the Emperor of Annam? Go ahead! Feel free. Don't hold anything back!'

'Well, I see you've done justice to the old wives' tales that have been drummed into you. That's a start.'

'You seem to be happy about what I've told you.'

'Of course. I've heard so many stories so far that I was beginning to wonder who was mad, me or the others.'

'Good. Well then, I hope to hear something reasonable from you. Let's hear it.'

'What I can tell you will, alas! only take a few words... Around two o'clock we were all gathered together in this room, except for Madame de Malèves, who stayed in her room, and Beaurieux, who had retired. We heard a shot. We all rushed upstairs, and, on breaking his door down, we found Beaurieux dead. Two hours later, Madame de Malèves, who was alone in the salon, was also shot. Her husband and the valet were not far away, at the junction of the entrance hall and the corridor, and they each entered through a different door, making it impossible for the murderer to escape. You can understand why, after that, the manor became empty.'

'I understand very well,' said Machaux. 'Where were the other inhabitants of the manor at that moment?'

'Dublard, Le Bellec and I were in the park; Jeanne Féral was found in the library, having fainted from fright. The cook and the chambermaid have disappeared since the death of Beaurieux.'

Machaux asked the journalist to clear up a few points of detail. After which:

'It's late,' he said, 'and I don't think I'll learn much more by staying here tonight. I prefer to go to the clinic at Saint-Germain. Maybe I can hear what Madame de Malèves has to say. I've a feeling she can give us some useful information.'

He thought for a few moments:

'After that, I'll see Monsieur Manceau, the juge d'instruction. It's likely that Le Parquet will come here tomorrow. I'll leave a couple of gendarmes here to guard the manor tonight. That will reassure your friends, perhaps.'

'Good grief! To do what? If the murderer is from another world, they won't be able to arrest him. And if he's made of normal flesh and blood, he'll surely be somewhere else, don't you think?'

'I don't think anything,' replied Machaux.

'Don't you think it's better to release all of us under surveillance?'

Machaux gave an ambiguous smile.

'There, there, my friend. I've got better things to do. Tomorrow is another day, as they say. Until then, if you stay overnight here in the manor, beware of ghosts.

'I gave instructions for the bodies of Monsieur Antoine de Malèves and your friend Beaurieux to be taken to the medical laboratory. I think it may already have been done. So, au revoir... and keep your head screwed on.'

After the policeman had left, Darlay wiped his moist neck.

'Has he really gone?' he asked himself. 'Anyway, it doesn't matter. Before tomorrow, he won't be thinking about the Emperor of China. That means twelve hours gained on him....'

***

Félix, still looking distraught, was waiting for him in the hallway.

'There's a telegramme, Monsieur. I'm sure it's from Monsieur le Baron. I'm afraid to ask...'

'Felix, old man, keep the faith. The operation was a success.'

'Thank goodness!'

The telegramme was concise:

"Operation completed. Bullet in lung not extracted, but danger seems over. Hélène is her old self.'

Darlay hastened to the library, where he hoped to find the rest of the guests. Dublard and Jeanne Féral were indeed there. The exhausted young woman was asleep in an armchair; far away from her, Dublard was absorbed in the study of a plan.

'So?' he asked in a low voice.

'Good news,' announced Darlay. 'Hélène has been saved.'

'Thank goodness!' said Dublard, just like Félix. 'There's already enough trouble here. Where's the bloody commissaire?'

'Gone. Do you know if the bodies have been taken away?'

'They have... I helped to bring....'

'Tomorrow,' said the reporter, 'all will become clear, perhaps.'

'How?'

'Antoine de Malèves and Beaurieux weren't able to speak, but Hélène will.'

'Well, that's true,' acknowledged Dublard. 'What shall we do whilst we're waiting?'

'Let's grab some food from the kitchen,' suggested Darlay, 'then get organised for the night; I don't suppose Mademoiselle Féral wants to spend the night alone in her room.'

The young woman woke up and, apprised of the situation, replied: 'Oh, no!'

'Then you can stay in Le Bellec's room; that way you'll be between my room and Dublard's.'

He was astonished. He'd thought that Jeanne Féral, convinced that he had been the cause of the attack against her friend Hélène, would have been hostile towards him... Yet she remained passive, almost distant. There was an expression of immense weariness on her face.

Served by Félix, they opened cans of preserves at one corner of the table and ate without talking. They gave the impression of hastening, without realising it, towards an unknown final outcome.

They went silently upstairs to their respective rooms, leaving Félix to disappear in the night to more hospitable places.

Darlay stretched out on his bed fully clothed; he wanted to reflect some more, but he soon dozed off with the bedside light still on.

Without being fully awake, he found himself standing up without understanding why, when the fourth death coup echoed in his ears.

***

Dublard and Darlay collided in front of Jeanne Féral's door. The lights from their open rooms shed some light on the corridor and, in the half-light, they could see each other's pale faces.

'You!'

'You!'

The animal satisfaction of finding themselves still alive, and the joy of each on seeing his friend safe and sound, gave way to the anguish of seeing the door between closed and silent.

'Jeanne! Jeanne!'

Together they rushed at the obstacle.

It's always the same thing. The door is well and truly locked from the inside. A panel cracks and yields. Darlay puts his arm inside, finds the key, juggles with the bolt.

The half-covered light from the bedside lamp shows Le Bellec's bed... Jeanne Féral is lying there, in a blue dressing gown, her black eyes open in a fixed stare....

XIII

A clue at last!

'Enough! Enough!' said Dublard in a strangled voice. 'I can't take any more!'

He staggered out of the room and disappeared into the shadows.

'Dublard!' shouted the journalist. 'Wait for me!'

Dublard must have heard the call, for the two men collided, arms extended, and gripped each other. The hostile silence of that night of terror embraced them and, stumbling down the stairs in panic, they fled the mysterious death and the suffocating atmosphere of that cursed place. In the deep corridor full of shadows, their hesitant steps echoed. It seemed to them that death was there, ambushing every turn, ready to descend upon them and bury them in darkness, prime witnesses to an enormous and incomprehensible tragedy. Tied to each other by a horror stronger than their reason, they reached the north door, fumbled to find the latch, and threw themselves outside. On the terrace, the fresh nocturnal air refreshed their sweaty brows as they continued to flee.

***

Pagnaud the farmer turned in his bed and heard the knocking on the door:

'Don't answer, Victor,' begged his wife.

'Need to take a look... don't worry, I won't show myself.'

He opened the window.

'Good God almighty, who's there? Don't come any closer, or I'll shoot!'

'Let us in, Pagnaud,' replied Darlay. 'Dublard's here as well.'

'You? At this hour? Just a minute, I'll come down. But what's going on, messieurs?' he asked, as he inched open the door.

'Nothing serious, rest assured,' replied the journalist, making a great effort to appear casual. 'Sorry to have woken you up; we wanted to know if we could use the room you made available for our friend Le Bellec. We're all alone in the manor, you understand, and...'

'Yes, you understand...,' repeated Dublard.

'Yes, I understand. In your place, I'd do the same thing. Come in messieurs, you'll sleep better here than back there. Whatever they say, it's no small thing to pass the night where strange things have happened... I'll show you to your room.'

The two friends followed the farmer up the wooden stairs. The run through the park had allowed them to recover their spirits, and in the darkness, their host was unable to observe any change in their expressions.

'Here we are,' anounced Pagnaud, opening a door. 'I'll turn the electricity on. You'll each have your own bed, you'll be fine, the mattresses have been changed from last year. Do you need anything else?'

'No thank you, this is everything we need.'

'Well, goodnight. See you in the morning.'

***

Good night!... That was a lot to ask! Dublard threw himself on one of the beds, pushing away the enormous red eiderdown. Now that he no longer needed to show constraint in front of the farmer, his fat body shook nervously and he puffed softly. Darlay walked around a pedestal table covered with fake cashmere, running his fingers through his hair. Suddenly, he seemed to make a decision and, going over to the water jug, he took several grand gulps of the stale, tepid water.

'Phew!' he said, refreshed.

His clarity of thought had returned. Now was the moment to take advantage of the novelist's disarray.

'Dublard,' he said solemnly, placing a hand on the other's shoulder, 'I want you to swear...'

'What?' murmured Dublard breathlessly.

'Swear that... alone in your room back there... you didn't have a pack of cards... You didn't—.'

'You're mad!' yelled Dublard, sitting bolt upright. 'I would have done it; yes, I was tempted, because I don't believe in those imbecilities, do you understand? But I didn't. It doesn't interest me... and, besides, I haven't got a pack of cards.'

'Don't shout, you'll disturb the farmers,' replied the journalist. 'I believe you.'

'That's lucky,' growled Dublard. 'You're going completely off the rails, my poor friend. I pity you!'

'Get lost!' retorted Darlay.

He sat down in front of the pedestal table and pulled a large piece of paper from his pocket. He picked up his pen. It wasn't worth trying to get to sleep, because he knew he couldn't. Better to get his ideas straight. For that, he should follow the tried and true method of committing his thoughts to paper. Then maybe a small light might appear at the end of the tunnel. He wrote:

First murder:
 Antoine de Malèves
 Saturday, at 7.20 p.m.
 Locked room, upper floor, east facade
 Bullet in right kidney

Far away at the time of the detonation: Dublard, Beaurieux,
 Le Bellec, Darlay, Jeanne Féral, Estelle

Close by, under each other's observation: Hélène de Malèves,
 Léontine

Unverifiable: Félix (to a certain degree), Pierre de Malèves
 (completely)

Clues: none

Second murder:
 Louis Beaurieux
 Sunday, at 2.00 p.m.
 Locked room, upper floor, south wing
 Bullet at the base of the skull

Far away at the time of the detonation: Dublard, Le Bellec, Darlay,
Jeanne Féral, Pierre de Malèves, Félix (smoking room),
Léontine (park), Estelle (village)

Unverifiable: Hélène de Malèves (in her room)

Clues: none

Third murder:
Hélène de Malèves
Sunday, at 3.30 p.m.
Salon, ground floor, east facade
Bullet in left lung

Far away at the time of the detonation: Darlay (roadhouse),
Le Bellec, Dublard (park)

Close by, under each other's observation: Pierre de Malèves, Félix

Unverifiable: Jeanne Féral (library), Estelle, Léontine (disappeared)

Clues: none

Fourth murder:
Jeanne Féral
Sunday, at 10.15 p.m.
Locked room, upper floor, east facade
Bullet in heart?

Far away at the time of the detonation: Pierre de Malèves (clinic)

Close by, under each other's observation: Darlay, Dublard

Unverifiable: Le Bellec, Félix, Estelle, Léontine (disappeared)

Clues: none

He read and re-read his paper. Really, it didn't help at all. Just supposing one of the inhabitants of the manor was the murderer (and, really, it seemed impossible to think it could be someone from the outside), it would have to be a different one each time, because every single one of them was out of the picture for at least one of the crimes. Furthermore, of the ten, three had been victims and the two last victims, Hélène and Jeanne, had been unverifiable (and therefore the most suspect) for the preceding murder.

Three others, Dublard, Le Bellec and Darlay were "materially" innocent for the first three murders. It was difficult to suspect, as authors of such brilliantly executed crimes, little Léontine or fat Estelle. That left Pierre de Malèves and Félix, who couldn't possibly have participated in the second murder, because they were in the smoking room; both of them unverifiable for the first case, they were together in the hall for the third. Objectively one might imagine their complicity. But for Beaurieux's death?

Dublard's voice sneered over the shoulder of his friend:

'It's not hard... it was Hélène who took responsibility and the two others who did the deed afterwards... Good, work, eh?'

His tone was so ironic that Darlay turned round with a weak smile.

'So, I see we're feeling better. You find my little exercise idiotic.'

'In its conclusions, yes, but it could have its uses. I see that at the foot of each case, you've written: "Clues: none". Well, my friend, that's not true, at least in the fourth case.'

'What do you mean?'

'Didn't you notice that in old de Malèves' and Beaurieux's rooms there was no odour?'

'No odour? Odour of what?'

'Wait... And that just now, in Jeanne's room, it smelt of gunpowder?'

'Hell's bells!' exclaimed the journalist. 'I'm kicking myself. Of course, now I think about it, it did smell of gunpowder. Strongly, in fact!'

'Yes. The shot was fired from inside the room.'

Darlay smacked himself on the head:

'And similarly for Hélène, there was an odour in the salon, but much less strong.'

'Personally, I didn't smell anything,' observed Dublard, 'but I came in much later. So now I'm going to share an idea I've just had, just to prove that I'm fully recovered.'

'I'm listening.'

'It's this: the bullet which hit Antoine de Malèves was certainly fired from a long way off, as the médecin légiste confirmed; the one that killed Beaurieux had perforated the base of the skull... So it must have had far greater momentum when it entered the room. Are you following me?'

'Keep going.'

'For Hélène, things changed: there was a slight odour of powder; For Jeanne, the odour was overwhelming. Conclusion: it appears as though, for each murder, *the killer kept coming closer....*'

'Well, well. You're not so stupid after all, Dublard! But why the killer? Why not just the weapon?'

'A weapon, without a finger on the trigger? In other words, automatic murders? A machine can't walk about, my friend; and in this case, *everything gets closer.*'

'You're overlooking another explanation: it's the victims who are getting closer to the machine...'

The journalist stopped, hesitating, then continued:

'But no, it's impossible: the murder sites are in a zig-zag line: three on the upper floor facing east, the first in the middle, the second towards the north, the third (the fourth chronologically) back towards the south... and Hélène's near-murder, facing west on the ground floor. No, it's not the victims advancing.'

'It's not the machine either, because there is no machine. Let's face it, the investigators were searching the whole afternoon. Machaux did the same thing. Death came in another way... Someone is doing the killing!'

'But nobody can be! It's like banging our heads against the walls!'

Darlay, his elbows on the table, shook his head between his hands. Now it was Dublard who was circling the table and who helped himself to a glass of water.

'We should have asked Pagnaud for some of his brandy. That would have helped.'

"How many men, through the ages, have found a truly original method of causing death?"

88

The journalist turned that sentence, that terrible sentence, over and over in his mind. No murderer... no weapon. Only a fool with a funnel on his head and... a bullet which kills. Death out of nowhere. That was the only reality... the only touchstone, illusory or not, the Emperor of China's coup; it always came back to that. Was it really he who had nearly killed Hélène? And was Dublard, as he turned around and around, asking himself, in his secret agony, whether he hadn't killed Beaurieux?

'Let's face it,' growled Darlay.

Dublard stopped:

'Face what?'

'Nothing. Keep going.'

Now Darlay was writing:

How many people knew how to invoke the Emperor of China's coup?

Before the first murder: one, Beaurieux.

Before the second murder, two: Dublard and Le Bellec.

Before the third murder, five: Dublard, Le Bellec, Darlay, Jeanne Féral, and Pierre de Malèves.

Before the fourth, the same. But Jeanne Féral is dead, Le Bellec has run away, Pierre de Malèves is by his wife's side in Saint-Germain. That only leaves Darlay and Dublard, each in his room.

'And it wasn't me,' murmurs Darlay.

Dublard was the only non-believer. Dublard, who had been present when the coup was first invoked. Dublard, who is still turning around, despite his fat body, and who refuses to accredit the hypothesis.

But when all's said and done, what does it prove, even if Dublard himself invoked the fourth murder? Even if he'd been reckless? More reckless than Darlay, who... It only went to show that it was indeed the Emperor of China who killed. And then what?

And if it wasn't Dublard? Another, unknown, who stumbled on the secret... but how? And why?

Another... or no one?

But if no one this time had done the "coup"... The death of Jeanne Féral?... That weapon which advances, advances a bit more with every bullet, which is in the room this time, with the hand holding it? It's the end of everything if we can't even grab the Emperor of China!

If we can't even envisage the incredible! unless... one last hope...

Supposing this time it's the same thing?

Darlay sits up.

'Dublard!'

'What?' says Dublard, still pacing about.

'I'm going back there.'

'You're go—you're crazy!'

Dublard opens his little eyes with their heavy eyelids as wide as he can, he raises his arms, he's going to kick up a fuss....

'Shut up! I said I'm going back there. I didn't ask you to accompany me.'

'But what's got into you?' says Dublard desperately. 'In the middle of the night? Do you want to get knocked off as well? All this is not enough for you? Do you think I'm going to let you go?'

'Listen, Dublard, I think I'm on to something. It's still very vague. I'm not exactly sure myself what I'm thinking, but there's something there... something, Dublard, since the moment you spoke of a strong odour. I need to go back to Jeanne's room... it can't wait until tomorrow.'

'You've got a lot of guts,' shudders the fat novelist.

But Darlay keeps talking and Dublard has stopped pacing; he listens with his hands on his stomach; he scratches his neck; he stops grumbling.

'Do you think so? Really?'

'Draw your own conclusions, Dublard; for that death, it's that or the devil. Your choice.'

'So it's got to be that, because I don't believe in the devil, at least when it comes to carrying a revolver.'

Dublard straightens up and swallows hard.

'I'm coming with you,' he says.

***

They leave the room quietly and descend the stairs furtively without disturbing the farmers in their room along the corridor. They are in the yard and manoeuvring the latch on the gate. What is that light between the trees? It's reddening like a fire... Dublard clutches his friend's arm.

'What's that?' he whispers.

'What's what?'

'Over there. Like a fire.'

'That's the moon rising, you idiot!'

'Ah. All that's missing is the twelve strokes of midnight.'

'You'll soon hear them in the village. In any case, the light helps. I'm amazed we found the farm on the way over here.'

'I'm lost,' confesses Dublard.

They make their way through woods quivering with nocturnal life.

'Seeing the light reminds me,' says the journalist calmly, 'we didn't turn the electricity off in the rooms when we left... So, don't be surprised.'

'It's a good job you reminded me.'

And indeed they do see the lights, filtered through the slats in the shutters. Dublard wishes he were somewhere else. A few hours earlier, it was he who pulled Le Bellec away. 'What a sinister building,' the coward had said....

'Are you coming?' grumbles Darlay.

They enter through the same door in the north wing through which they had left, and this time the journalist turns on a switch. The light from the globe of frosted glass chases away all mystery; there is the hall, wide and high but peaceful, and there is the plain, open stairwell. Darlay takes a step up and Dublard follows. Come what may! There's no going back. There is the half-broken door. After a moment's hesitation, they are in the room.

And there before them... After all, it is the enduring picture of death. They stop and look.

Ah! gentle Le Bellec, is this what you foresaw this morning from your own bed....

In a blink, Darlay controls his memories; this is it. The body is stretched out on the couch, the head slightly backwards; the eyes stare at the ceiling, and the arms are extended away from the body. The left hand, long and fine, reposes on the sheet, the right is half-hidden on the other side, between the couch and the wall. Darlay throws a scarf over the troubling face, then pulls the couch sideways.A muffled thud on the wood floor, at the foot of the wall... He squeezes between and leans down....

'Well, well,' he says, with a note of triumph.

91

It's a heavy revolver, British-made, with a solid grip and touches of rust.

'Ah!' exclaims Dublard in a hoarse voice. 'You were right.'

Darlay leans over the corpse.

'Look, Dublard.'

He pulls the dressing-gown gently open. The hard white breast bears the characteristic traces, tattoos of powder. Yes, the weapon was so far forward that it touched the skin....

'It's so stupid. My God, so stupid,' murmurs the journalist.

... What is stupid? That Jeanne Féral killed herself, or that Darlay hadn't understood right away? Did the two of them need to be upset that they hadn't probed more deeply?

Darlay picks up the weapon and examines it.

'Nothing in the chamber or the barrel. The last bullet was for her.'

'But why, why?' whispers Dublard. 'She wasn't the one who....'

'Too soon to draw any conclusions, my friend.'

'And suppose it's been staged?' says Dublard. 'Yes, that's it, someone put the weapon in her hand, after...'

Darlay shrugs his shoulders:

'We were twenty seconds too late. That said, the weapon would have had to have jumped into her hand by itself, and it's not a magical instrument. And here's the proof!'

He picks up a sheet of mauve writing-paper from the washstand. There are two lines on it in the young woman's elegant handwriting. He reads them out:

'*"To my great misfortune, I have solved the puzzle of the Emperor of China. Adieu.*

J.FÉRAL"'

XIV

Darlay has an idea

"The simpler it is, the less one thinks about it."
"A conjuring trick to end all conjuring tricks."

Beaurieux, a gadfly, had imagined it. Jeanne Féral had solved it in less than twenty-four hours... And neither was extraordinary. Intelligent, no doubt, but even so!...

And Darlay, not a genius perhaps, but all the same... Was he going to remain impotent in the face of this trivial mystery?

And Jeanne Féral killed herself because....

'I'll give myself until dawn,' decided the journalist.

He had gone downstairs with Dublard to the library, each with a blanket to cover himself, each feigning sleep in an armchair whilst he meditated. A lampstand with a large shade created a circle of light on a console which mirrored the facets of an ornamental chest, and the rest was darkness.

'Dublard,' murmured Darlay, his eyes closed, 'you who excel at unravelling the subtle threads of mysteries...'

'Huh,' said the fat Dublard, not stirred from his evident lethargy by the flattery .

'You've been in the habit of creating impossible situations and leaving the solutions for later.'

'Certainly,' replied Dublard in a purring voice. 'Right now I don't know how the murderer got in, but it will come to me. It's just a matter of routine.'

'Good. Suppose you were to write Beaurieux's story. Suppose you were seduced by the improbability of... what he did... into saying: "I'll find a solution which makes the readers happy."'

'No,' said Dublard.

'What do you mean, no?'

'I respect my readers. Granted that I string them along and I arrange things a little, you understand. But there are some things I won't do. I

93

have a horror of the marvellous psychic power, it's too easy... There's no human explanation for the Emperor of China's coup, therefore I can't even imagine the supposition you describe. The Emperor of China's coup doesn't exist.'

Still the same stubbornness—the voluntary blindfold. Good old Dublard, whose subconscious even refuses to participate in the murder of his friend.

'And yet,' observed Darlay, 'Jeanne Féral solved it and killed herself... Do you contest the testimony of someone about to kill themselves?'

'One can, even at the moment one kills oneself, maintain a theatrical attitude and seek to preserve appearances. You know very well why Jeanne Féral killed herself.'

'I know,' sighed the journalist. 'At least I can make out several motives which no doubt add to one another: elation, disappointment, remorse.'

'And fear of tomorrow,' added Dublard. 'Tomorrow Hélène will talk, or at least Jeanne imagines she will, which amounts to the same thing. The suicide signs the crime.'

'Dublard... Do you really think that it was Jeanne who shot Hélène?'

In the darkness, the fat fellow nodded his head:

'And you think so, too. The stage setting was cleverly done. She knew how to exploit the atmosphere of terror and mystery surrounding Beaurieux's practical joke. You must admit that, for several hours, none of us was capable of thinking rationally.'

'Frankly, Dublard, I'd like to hear you explain how you deduced the role Jeanne Féral played.'

'I only understood after her death which, I repeat, proved her culpability as much as the weapon in her possession. And, if we hadn't all been obsessed by the extravagances, we would have suspected the truth straight away. Think about it: when Hélène was wounded, her husband was with Félix in the hall, each providing the other with an alibi and controlling access to the salon. Le Bellec, you and I were in the park. I wasn't so far from the terrace that I couldn't see it was deserted. Consequently, the attack could only have come from the direction of the library, and who should be in the library but Jeanne Féral, totally unobserved.'

'Brilliant, except for the minor detail that there's no connecting door between the library and the salon.'

'That did dawn on me after I formulated my theory,' said Dublard placidly. 'But now it's my turn to tell you it's that or thedevil, because clearly, Pierre, with the help of Félix, didn't... Is this part of the manor very old?'

'Sixteenth century, like all the ground floor. The upper floor was redone, I believe, before 1870. What? You're not going to talk to me about a secret passage, I hope. That's like a cheap serial, Dublard. And anyway, how would she have known about it?'

'No, I was thinking of something else. In any case, if my idea is wrong, there's always the possibility of patting the walls in search of a well-hidden button; but maybe it's much simpler than that. I don't want you to sneer.'

'I promise not to sneer. I'm listening.'

'Well what about the fireplace? Isn't the salon fireplace built back-to-back with the one here? Suppose the back of the hearth were movable?'

'We can always take a look,' said Darlay, interested.

Disengaging himself from the cover, he got up and went to turn on the electricity. The two bulbs in the ceiling lit up. Under the white, diffused light, the monumental fireplace appeared out of the darkness.

Dublard had also got up and joined him. Now the two men, bending down in the hearth, examined the cast iron backplate. Classical figures were embossed on the shining surface: Pomona, with her procession of lovers bearing baskets in a framework of vines.

The journalist tapped with his fingers, seeking, without great conviction, to release some secret mechanism.

'Well,' he said, 'that was easy.'

By placing his hands on either side of the centre and pushing in opposite directions, the two halves separated, revealing the salon hearth.

'Bravo, Dublard!'

'Thank Alexandre Dumas, because I read about something similar in one of his books... I remember it vaguely from a childhood reading. Apparently it happened quite often in the sixteenth and seventeenth centuries. It was a way of going from one room to another. She must have found it by chance, or read about it in one of the books here. So, when she was sure that you were going to the lodge to try out Beaurieux's trick, because you took a red mat, she got rid of me and Le Bellec by sending us out after you.'

'But if you'd arrived in time and prevented me from invoking the coup, how would she have known, in order to defer it to another occasion?'

'Bah! She decided to go for broke. She took the revolver, which she must have hidden here; there's no shortage of hiding places. Under the cushion of her armchair, perhaps... She manoeuvred the backplates, took a quick look to check that Hélène was alone, reached forward, and fired.'

'However,' said Darlay, picking up the thread, 'she realised (or imagined) that Hélène had seen her, either directly or in the mirror opposite the fireplace, so that when she survived, she—Jeanne—was lost.'

'Too bad for her,' sneered Dublard. 'Otherwise, after a few months, she could have consoled Pierre... and become baronne!'

On that funeral oration, the fat fellow extinguished the lights and the library fell dark again. Each of them returned to his armchair, his cover and his meditation.

'Dublard,' said Darlay again, after a long moment of silence.

'Now what is it?'

'In your opinion, was Jeanne Féral responsible for the other murders?'

'Who knows? Note that it would have been stupid. What did she have against old Malèves and Beaurieux? But anything's possible.'

'But even so, not that. She was with me each time, remember?'

'I didn't say it was her. I don't know anything.'

'So, let me ask my question again:

"You who excel at unravelling the subtle threads, etc., what explanation would you give for the two first murders, in one of your detective novels?"'

'In a novel, that's easy! I've already shown Le Bellec how, in the case of old de Malèves, you yourself could have done it.'

'Thanks, that was niceof you. I'd be curious...'

'Later! It's just by way of saying it's not difficult. I would have Pierre firing from some point in the corridor at the old man, who then shuts the door behind him. For the second, I would have Hélène do

96

the job, because only she had the time. As for the motive—.'

'You're odious.'

'I'm not odious, I'm simply objective. And you're becoming annoying, you keep talking about novels. It's not about the real Pierre and Hélène, our friends. In reality, there's no argument.'

'So, nothing? You're happy to leave things unexplained?'

'You're going to throw the Emperor of China at me again,' grumbled Dublard, 'but there's nothing more to say. Listen, my friend, just be patient. An hour ago, we were neck-deep in mystery, and now two of the murders have been solved, very logically. So, for heaven's sake, let's stay logical. Let's assume that the two first murders can also be explained the same way, despite appearances, without magical intervention. Do you know what? Let's try and get some sleep. We'll be able to think more clearly in the morning.'

'Maybe you're right. Goodnight.'

***

"The simpler it is..."

Darlay, his eyes closed, concentrated his thoughts. He'd had Le Bellec describe in great detail how Beaurieux had gone about it; he'd witnessed Dublard's demonstration in the smoking room and he himself denying what seemed impossible; and, alone in the roadhouse, he'd repeated the experiment... But, if he accepted Dublard's position, the Emperor of China's coup (that idiotic phrase needed to be changed) had not worked, because it was Jeanne Féral who....

And it suddenly dawned forcefully on Darlay that Jeanne Féral had not lied when she said she'd solved the puzzle; she could only profit from the mystery after having rendered it ineffective!

He soliloquized:

'If she hadn't already understood the Emperor of China's coup, she wouldn't have let me take the red mat without a protest; in any case, even if one supposes that death could have struck her, just as any other occupant of Breule, she could have escaped to the park.

'But suppose she'd been paralysed by fright?

'Then she wouldn't have been able, thirty seconds later, to...

'Yes, if she'd been unaware of the secret, she would have prevented me instead of sending someone after me when there wasn't time. Didn't I do the same thing with Machaux? When he complained about the nonsense being peddled, didn't I agree in order to avoid the policeman coming to the demonstration, and maybe provoking another catastrophe?

'Jeanne Féral knew the secret. She disarmed the killing machine, because she had the revolver. Even better, thanks to that secret, she was able to know, from the library, that, over in the lodge, I had launched the invocation. Whatever Dublard thinks, she wouldn't have acted without being sure. At two hundred metres, without any liaison, beyond the mirror of water and the flower beds, she had seen!

'But how? Was it because I came out suddenly to...'

***

'Ah!' he exclaimed, sitting up, struck by a stunning revelation.

His brain was in turmoil because of the emotion, like a film running at breakneck speed... he recalled Beaurieux's strangely turned-up nose and the strange sight of Dublard under his handkerchief, knotted in all four corners... Le Bellec's bulging eyes and the fragile figure of Hélène de Malèves on the carpet... and the incomprehensible phrases.

"It could take months to modify that phrase..."

"Try not to put the funnel on the head... start with a handkerchief, then, little by little, nothing..."

'My God!' he thought. 'That must be it. It could only be that. And no way of controlling it until daylight...'

XV

'The murderer is in the room...'

Gourvet, the gardener-caretaker, dipped his bread in his black coffee with an obstinate air and chewed slowly without raising his head. His wife circulated around him in the small, bright kitchen whose window overlooked the road; a canary sang in the cage near the door, dazzled by a ray of sunshine.

'Well, Ernest,' asked his wife, 'what are we going to do?'

She was a small, rather ugly brunette. She pressed the table with shaking hands and turned her anxious face to her husband.

'For sure,' said Gourvet slowly, 'we're going to have to make a decision.'

'You've heard Félix, there's a lot of strange goings-on. The police don't see anything, because... I'm telling you, Ernest, all that... all that...'

Leaning over her husband, she spoke in a low, hesitant voice.

'There's a curse there. I've read stories about such happenings. I tell you the manor is haunted... yes... as they say, bewitched. Those crimes come from another world... that's why the police don't understand anything.'

'It does seem like it,' conceded Gourvet.

'I'll tell you what I think, myself. Something happened last night. Félix doesn't know what, but I'm sure he suspects something. I'm telling you there's death in that manor... death... death... and we're all going to go. All of us!'

She burst into tears and clutched her husband, who got up and pushed his bowl away.

'Look here, Rosa,' he said irritably, 'you're giving yourself ideas. First of all, we don't live in the manor. So?'

'Do you think that matters? Revolver shots which happen by themselves, couldn't they strike anyone? Us, in our kitchen, or the little one in his bed? What would you say, eh, if you found him dead in his bed now? No, Ernest, we can't stay here... we have to leave!'

'Listen, Rosa, this morning all the messieurs of the police arrive, and the juge d'instruction and his aides... what do you think could happen?'

'Magic doesn't care about your juge d'instruction! And there could very well be a death before then. At least let me leave with the little one, Ernest... we can go to your aunt. I can't take it any more, I can't.'

'Someone's knocking at the door,' interrupted Gourvet. 'Leave, so they don't see you in that state. All right, we'll see about it.'

'Are you there, Gourvet?' It was Darlay's voice. 'What's going on? Are you barricading yourself in, now?' he added as he came in, Gourvet having unbolted the door.

'It's Rosa,' explained the other. 'She's nervous, and with good reason. Tell me, Monsieur, did anything bad happen last night?'

The journalist shrugged his shoulders. His features were drawn and his eyes gleamed with a vague air of satisfaction.

'Come now, Gourvet! No, nothing bad happened. It's over, do you understand... over!'

'I'd like to believe you, Monsieur. But who knows? What makes you think so?'

'I've no time to explain. It's eight o'clock. Tell me, could I find a car in the village for an urgent errand?'

'I think so. There's a mechanic in the square, Jeantard, who has a decent old banger which he runs as a taxi sometimes.'

'Good, thanks,' said the reporter as he left, 'and I'm telling you, it's over... over!'

'Over?' murmured Gourvet, in a tone mixed with hope and doubt.

Darlay almost ran along the road. He didn't feel tired, despite two nights without sleep, and the elation he experienced at decisive moments made his brain clear and his muscles supple. It only took a few minutes for him to cover the distance between the manor and the nearby village, whose church steeple seemed to pierce the sky.

The mechanic agreed willingly and wheeled out an old but robust saloon car.

'Where do you want to go, Monsieur?'

'To Mantes,' replied the journalist, 'with pedal to the floor!'

The automobile roared to life and quickly reached the desired cruising speed. Darlay, regularly jolted on the rear banquette, began to lay out his plan.

'First knock on the right doors,' he said to himself, 'the commissariat, then the mairie if necessary. If there's a chance to use official channels, that would be the goal. Then we'll see.'

But, on arrival in Mantes, as the vehicle was crossing the railway tracks, he uttered a cry of satisfaction.

'Ah! That's a bit of luck! If I'm not mistaken, there's a merry-go-round with wooden horses over there. That's better than all the commissariats! Turn left, my man, onto the boulevard and stop next to the merry-go-round.'

'Very well, Monsieur,' said the driver, without emotion.

It was a modest little merry-go-round, covered in tarpaulin; one for small children. In the dark, behind the red-striped canvas, would be pink pigs suspended on copper rods pulling chariots in the form of swans. The barrel organ was not playing, nor were the solemn babies riding under the watchful eyes of their mothers. There was only Darlay, walking around outside, with no baby to watch, trying to find his way. Two silent caravans stood on either side of the merry-go-round. He walked aroundthem... nobody. Then he made the decision to knock on the door of one of them.

'What is it?' asked a husky male voice.

'It's about an important job.'

The door opened to reveal a bearded giant in his shirt-sleeves. Jeantard, the mechanic, didn't hear what transpired. Darlay had gone inside.

A quarter-of-an-hour later, he emerged wearing an expression of triumph. The giant closed the door behind him, scratching his head.

'How far to Vernon?'

'About twenty-five kilometres.'

'Let's go... Still pedal to the floor... Try to get there before half-past nine.'

Nine twenty-five. Vernon. The small town was bustling; Monday was market day. The car found its way and stopped in front of the hospital. Darlay argued with the receptionist.

'It's not visiting hours,' objected the latter.

But the journalist was used to such small obstacles; he knew how to overcome them easily. A small discussion with the head doctor who had just arrived. A discreet flash of his pass, and he was in the men's dormitory, in front of number fourteen.

'Monsieur Jérôme Péquin?'

'That's me. What can I do for you?'

'I've come to see you on behalf of Grandet, the owner of the merry-go-round.'

'Grandet? About what?'

Jérôme Péquin raised himself on one elbow. He was an old man with hollow cheeks and a shaven head.

'Excuse me,' he said, 'I can hardly move ever since I broke my hip, and I'm stuck in this damned apparatus which holds me and won't let go. I'm sure I'm going to kick the bucket here.'

'Don't talk like that,' said Darlay cheerfully. 'I'm the bearer of news which I think will give you pleasure.'

'News which will give me pleasure,' grumbled the old man. 'I doubt it.'

'Maybe you can guess. But first I must remind you of something.'

Darlay sat down close to the bed and leant towards the invalid's ear. He murmured:

'And the Emperor of China be damned!'

The old man's face lit up. A comic grimace crossed his features, then he nodded melancholically without looking at Darlay.

'Ah!' he sighed. 'Those were the days.'

At half-past ten, the journalist ran out of the hospital.

'To Breule!' he said to the mechanic.

'Pedal to the floor, I assume?'

'Of course.'

At quarter-past eleven, the car was asking for entrance to the park. Gourvet's wife showed her frightened face and came to open the gate. Shortly after, Darlay went through the main entrance and into the hall. A gendarme was guarding the door; he recognised the journalist from the last two days.

'We were wondering what had become of you, Monsieur. Le Parquet has been here for nearly an hour... Everyone is in the dining room.'

'I'm on my way.'

He pushed open the dining room door.

'A big get-together,' he thought.

Everyone was indeed there: the examining magistrate seated at the big table leafing through his papers; the public prosecutor standing by the fireplace; the clerk with the pen between his teeth; Machaux in discussion; an inspector... and then Dublard, the cook Estelle, Félix the valet, the caretaker Gourvet, the little lady's maid Léontine, and even the farmer Pagnaud... all talking at once.

There was a sudden silence as Darlay entered, and all eyes turned towards him. He stepped forward with a smile, looked at all present,and seemed to be searching with his eyes under the table and then the sideboard.

'The murderer is in the room!' he announced.

The declaration, announced with a firm assurance, had the effect of a bomb thrown into the room. The magistrate, who, before Darlay's entrance, had been listening with interest to Commissaire Machaux's explanation, and who—having formed a firm opinion—was about to come to a clear conclusion, was the first to get his breath back.

'Who is this monsieur?' he asked, vexed at being deprived of the opportunity to impose his will.

'Darlay, reporter at *L'Informateur*,' replied the journalist.

Commissaire Machaux whispered a few words in the magistrate's ear. The latter's attitude changed.

'Very well,' he said stiffly. 'Let's hear the sensational revelations of Monsieur le journaliste.'

The magistrate's tone did nothing to please Darlay, whose own character was difficult enough.

'Monsieur le journaliste will start with a few verifications,' he said curtly. 'If you care to listen, you won't be obliged to hear long explanations.'

Monsieur Manceau's face turned brick red. He was about to reply sharply when another whisper from Commissaire Machaux calmed him once more. Dublard seemed to be enormously amused. Darlay addressed him in turn:

'Could you find me a red mat and pack of cards?'

'Right away, old boy.'

'And a funnel as well.'

'Right-ho,' said the novelist as he left.

When he returned, Darlay placed the funnelon his head and placed the king of spades on the mat between the red aces.

'What's all this tomfoolery?' muttered the magistrate.

'Leave the door open and be prepared to follow me... fast,' said the journalist, ignoring the remark.

He took the king of spades, threw it on the floor and shouted:

'And the Emperor of China be damned!'

So saying, he rushed out of the roo Magistrates, policemen, witnesses, now caught up in the excitement, pursued him madly.

Dublard and Machaux reached the dining room door at the same time and collided. The policeman disengaged himself first, quite forcefully, and ran to catch up with the others. Dublard tried to do the same thing, but bumped into the fat Estelle and both fell over. The novelist decided to give up the chase, helped the cook to her feet and walked calmly outside. The noise of voices indicated which way to go.

When he arrived at the entrance to the tower, Darlay showed the policemen a rope hanging all the way to the ground.

'By pulling on that,' he said, 'the shot is fired.'

He led them to the floor above. In front of an arrow slit, they could see a wooden framework to which the rope was attached.

'That was where the revolver was housed,' said Darlay triumphantly.

Led by the journalist, magistrates and policemen next visited the rooms of M. Antoine de Malèves and Beaurieux. With the help of pertinent remarks by Dublard, Darlay succeeded in shining the light on the events in Breule manor.

XVI

Shining the light

The gravel on the terrace crackled as Pierre de Malèves swung his large car onto it... Darlay appeared in the front doorway like a host greeting his guests. The two men embraced:

'So? She's been saved?'

'Yes! Saved! The surgeon says she can leave in a couple of days. But poor Jeanne! It's terrible. When I got your call this morning, I didn't understand anything. Is she upstairs?'

'No. You'll understand in a moment. And then we have to forget everything, my friend, as if it's all been a nightmare. Yesterday afternoon you left a place where panic reigned and the menace of death was everywhere; twenty-four hours later, you come home to a place where mystery has been banished!'

'But how, Lucien? By what miracle? I have to appear in court tomorrow.'

'A pure formality, believe me, to close the case officially. Everything was cleared up this morning. It was a lively session. Monsieur Manceau the judge was there, the deputy public prosecutor, Machaux, an inspector, the clerk and several sidekicks. Everyone has left. But here's Dublard.'

Dublard came running in from the park, preceded by the fox terrier which, catching sight of its master, barked joyfully.

'And Le Bellec?' asked de Malèves.

'Pfft!' said Dublard. 'Monsieur took the train to Paris yesterday, leaving his luggage behind. He'll be back. But let's go inside. Darlay has been terrific, you know.'

'Come now, Dublard.'

'Yes, terrific. If you could have seen him this morning, holding forth to the law... What a spectacle! You have to take your hat off to him.'

'Dublard did half the work.'

'My friends, I repeat I don't understand anything. Please explain.'

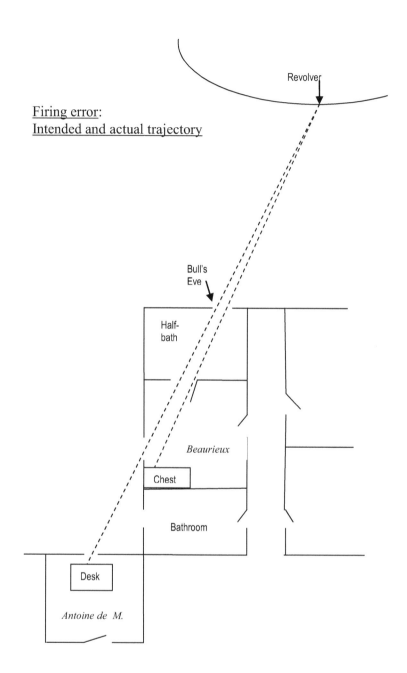

Firing error:
Intended and actual trajectory

Revolver

Bull's
Eye

Half-
bath

Beaurieux

Chest

Bathroom

Desk

Antoine de M.

106

'Let's go into the smoking room,' suggested Darlay.

The journalist started by telling de Malèves about the events of the preceding night and how, following Jeanne's suicide, Dublard and he had confirmed the young woman's guilt in the attempted murder of Hélène.

'But why did she do it?' asked the bewildered lord of the manor.

'Alas! my poor friend, you and Hélène took an adventuress to your bosoms. Granted she was a childhood friend of your wife, but they hadn't kept in touch for several years, and you hadn't even met her until a few weeks ago, I believe?'

'No. Who would have thought?'

'She played the part of a sweet young woman very well. It could well be that when she first arrived here, her only thought was to get free lodging for a while. Be that as it may, she adapted to her new circumstances very quickly. She obviously felt that she would make a very presentable Baronne de Malèves one day.'

'The devil she did!'

'Don't think about her any more. Justice has been done. This morning, I arranged for her body to be taken away. And now,' continued the journalist hurriedly, 'I will explain to you how Antoine de Malèves and Beaurieux met their deaths. It's important to know that Jeanne Féral had indeed cracked the secret of the Emperor of China's coup.'

'So it was true!'

'Yes, it was true! Listen: poor Beaurieux had stumbled upon an outlandish secret. He had found (I'll tell you how in a minute) a way to set off any kind of apparatus, for example a bell or a siren, at a distance... and had had the very unfortunate idea of playing a practical joke in order to mystify Dublard.

'The trick would also allow him to pull the trigger of a revolver and, having found a vintage one, he constructed a wooden framework to house it in the arrow slit of the old tower, right opposite the bull's-eye in his bathroom. As he was leaving his room the day before yesterday, in the afternoon, he made a point of telling Dublard and Le Bellec that his alarm clock—placed on his chest of drawers—was precisely synchronised with their watches. It was undoubtedly intended to be the "victim" of the joke. Once the bull's-eye and the door between the bathroom and Beaurieux's room were left open, the alarm clock could be shattered by a bullet at a time determined by Dublard, a time recorded on the demolished mechanism. After which, all Beaurieux would have to do would be to close the bull's-eye by means of a thread hanging down from it, which he could surreptitiously manoeuvre from outside, behind the kitchen, and Dublard would be presented with a mysterious "murder" which our imaginative friend would defy him to explain.

'Unfortunately, Beaurieux had failed to aim the weapon properly, or it had not been securely fixed, because the bullet deviated slightly to the right. It broke a pane of glass in the window and continued on, killing Antoine de Malèves in his room. Would you care to explain, Dublard, how the old man could have been struck, even though we found the shutters closed?'

'Well, take a look at this,' said Dublard. 'I found it below your uncle's window yesterday morning.'

'What is it?' asked the lord of the manor. 'Why, it's the ring from an electric light bulb!'

'Precisely, and I constructed my chain of logic starting with this small piece of metal. Do you remember Darlay talking about the cook's curious testimony? She was the only one to have heard a small detonation which she compared to a paper bag being burst?'

'Well, I'll be... !' exclaimed Pierre. 'I understand: it was the light bulb exploding on the paving stones!'

'Undoubtedly. Now we can reconstruct the fatal sequence of events: the light bulb illuminating your uncle's room suddenly went out, possibly because of a surge in voltage. Plunged into shadow, the old man naturally opened the window and the shutters to give him some light. Darkness continued to fall, so he unscrewed the bulb, which he could reach by raising his arms, and calmly threw it out of the window. Then he took another bulb he had stored somewhere and screwed that in.

'It was at the precise moment that he finished that operation, with arms and body extended, that he was struck in the kidney... Being hard of hearing, he hadn't noticed the detonation, made even fainter by the angle of the south wing, so he thought for a moment that he'd just pulled a muscle. So he closed the shutters and the window... and collapsed soon thereafter from an internal haemorrhage. Does that make sense?'

Pierre de Malèves nodded in approval. Darlay took up the story:

'When Beaurieux realised the terrible consequences of his practical joke, he was, quite naturally, horrified. Luckily for him, nobody seemed to suspect him in any way. He hurried back to his room and saw the broken pane; he resolved to eliminate all traces of his involvement. In his panic, he didn't think to, or didn't dare to dismantle the infernal machine... He concentrated on replacing the glass. It wasn't difficult: all the necessary material was stored in the outbuildings; it was usually Gourvet who took care of such matters. Beaurieux managed to smuggle glass and putty into his room, probably at night, and managed to repair the damage.

'The following morning, he would certainly have wanted to recover the revolver, but he would have had to go near the body of Antoine de Malèves, now lying in the base of the tower awaiting the autopsy, and he obviously hadn't the courage to do so.

'Now Beaurieux's own death isn't hard to explain: our poor friend was in his room when the second Emperor of China's coup occurred. Naturally, he never dreamt that one of us would repeat the insanity of the day before, and besides he had taken the precaution of removing the pack of cards from the lodge. As he collapsed, killed on the spot, his body twisted towards the bathroom door. As it slammed shut, the draught thus created caused the bull's-eye to shut in turn, creating a second locked room murder.

'Whilst I was examining the room later, I was so emotionally upset that I failed to notice that the window had only recently been installed and the putty was not yet dry. Commissaire Machaux, however, did notice, three hours later. When we saw each other, however, I appeared to have lost my sang-froid. He judged I would be of little use in the investigation, so he kept that information to himself without finding an explanation. What more can I say?'

'You can tell us the key to the puzzle!' retorted Pierre de Malèves. 'All of what you said is beautifully reasoned, but how did Beaurieux manage to fire a revolver remotely by means of a pack of cards?'

'That's just it, old man, he didn't manage anything at a distance. The pack of cards and the phrase possessed no magical powers . It's much more simple than that... *The simpler it is, the less one thinks about it."*

'You're getting me really upset, Lucien!'

'Haven't you understood yet that it was an accomplice who fired? The cards, the phrase and all the rest were just a pre-arranged signal.'

'You're trying to make a fool of me. An accomplice blessed with such speed and... invisibility to match. It's impossible.'

'And yet it's true, Pierre. The accomplice is actually right here, next to you.'

And, whilst de Malèves stared at them in disbelief, Darlay hastened to add:

'He's even under your chair. Come out from your hiding-place, Mister Buck, and explain to your master how you did it....'

Pierre de Malèves, struck dumb, stared at his little fox terrier who, aroused by the journalist's call, had come out wagging his tail joyfully, begging for a hug.

'A few months ago, you found him wandering in the park, half-dead from hunger, I believe?'

'That's right,' the other replied. 'All I knew about him was the name inscribed on his collar.'

'Well, sometime before that, towards the end of our stay last year, Beaurieux decided to take a bicycle trip to Mantes. Whilst wandering around, he took it into his head to visit one of those little circuses where an entire family performs under a canvas stretched between two caravans to an audience seated on wooden benches.

'There was an old clown doing tricks with trained dogs. One of his acts involved him, ridiculously dressed and wearing a funnel upside-down on his head, placing three cards on a red mat. When he threw the king of spades to the ground and shouted, "And the Emperor of China be damned!" Mister Buck came out wearing a mandarin's coat and hat. Walking on his hind legs, he pulled on a hanging rope, which caused a tiny cannon to fire and the clown to run away. Are you beginning to understand?

'How did the fox terrier end up here? I found out this morning by carrying out a little investigation in the region. Last night, when I had the revelation that the accomplice could only be Mister Buck, I suddenly remembered that Beaurieux had told me last year, on his return from Mantes: "I've been to see some clever dogs." That's all he'd said, and I'd forgotten about it until it suddenly came to me.

'So this morning I resolved to find out more about that dog trainer and went to Mantes, where I planned to make enquiries about travelling fairs at the mairie and the gendarmerie. I was saved the trouble, because I noticed a children's merry-go-round. You know that people who run travelling fairs know everything about each other. The owner of the merry-go-round told me the dog trainer's name was Jérôme Péquin, who had worked in a little circus there in Mantes at the time Beaurieux had visited. The poor man had had an accident afterwards and should still be in the hospital at Vernon.

'And that's where I found him half-an-hour later. The poor old man is alone in the world and was still lamenting the fact that his three dogs had been sent to the pound after his transfer to the hospital. I still don't know how one of them managed to escape and eventually find refuge in Breule. In any case, I promised him I'd return soon and told him about "the Emperor of China's coup."'

'That's fantastic!'

'Now,' continued Darlay, 'we can make some assumptions which will be pretty close to the truth. When Beaurieux came along with the rest of us to the lodge this year, he found the dog which you had adopted as his new master... He probably searched his memory for some time after hearing the name Mister Buck. After he remembered, he kept quiet about it, realising that he might be able to play a good trick on his friends at some point.

'After getting into the dog's good graces, he proceeded to accustom it to pull on a rope in the tower whilst he, Beaurieux, went farther and farther away with his pack of cards. It was merely a question of patience. The dog was able to get into the tower, even when the door was shut, by the badly-fitting cellar window you know about... Once inside, he could pull on the rope from the dark corner at the foot of the staircase and activate the revolver on the floor above.

'Immediately after the fatal shot which had caused the death of Antoine de Malèves, Mister Buck slipped out of the roadhouse without attracting the attention of Dublard or Le Bellec, but Jeanne Féral, who was walking to the manor with me, must have seen the dog and noticed that it went into the tower. The following day, in the smoking room, whilst Dublard was recreating the invocation, she noticed that when Félix brought the coffee in, the fox terrier came in as well. She very astutely connected those two observations to work out what had happened. Yesterday, during the afternoon, she went into the tower undaunted and took the revolver.

111

'As soon as Jeanne Féral saw me take one of the red mats from the library, she reasoned correctly that I was going to try to understand Beaurieux's puzzle and decided to take advantage. She had seen Mister Buck follow me. This time the dog couldn't play a role in any murder, but by running out of the lodge, he provided proof that I must have pronounced the magic phrase.

'As for me, I saw the fox terrier run away, but I thought he'd suddenly detected the presence of a stranger, so I followed him. Needless to say, he was too fast for me, so I didn't see him go into the tower where, for once, he didn't unleash a shot... It was only later that I understood.'

'My God!' murmured Pierre de Malèves, 'How complicated this all was, yet how simple. To think that we really believed that occult forces were responsible!'

'It's an unfortunate human tendency,' concluded Dublard philosophically. 'But there is one consolation in all this sadness: luckily for the police and for mankind in general, death always comes from somewhere....'

THE END

APPENDIX: THE FRENCH GOLDEN AGE

To my knowledge, there is no accepted definition of a French locked room Golden Age, but—despite the isolated activities of Gaston Leroux in 1907-08; Boileau-Narcejac as a team in the 1950s; Martin Méroy in the 1960s; and the one-man Golden Age of Paul Halter starting in the 1980s—it is hard to deny that the preponderance of authors and titles occurred between 1930 and 1948. Much of the information below comes from the excellent bibliography *1000 Chambres Closes,* by Roland Lacourbe *et al*.

1930 saw the appearance of Pierre Véry's *Le Testament de Basil Crookes* (The Testament of Basil Crookes), and 1948 was the year that Thomas Narcejac's *La Mort est du voyage* (Death on Board) won the *Grand Prix du Roman d'aventures*, France's international award for mystery fiction (He and Boileau met at Narcejac's award dinner.)

The period between those years saw three prolific authors: Maurice Leblanc, Noël Vindry and the Belgian Stanislas-André Steeman; Pierre Boileau and Thomas Narcejac writing separately; and many of what Roland Lacourbe calls "meteors of the night"—authors who produced one or two books in a very short period, then disappeared from sight.

Maurice Leblanc is best known for his short stories featuring ArsèneLupin, but his gentleman thief also appears in two novels: La *Barre-y-va* (The Barre-y-va) in 1932, and *La Femme aux deux sourires* (The Woman With Two Smiles) in 1933.

Of Steeman's more than thirty novels, five contained locked room puzzles: *Six homes morts* (Six Dead Men) and *La Nuit du 12 au 13* (The Night of the 12th and 13th) in 1931; *Zéro* (Zero) in 1932; *L'Ennemi sans visage* (The Enemy Without a Face) in 1934; and *L'Infaillible Silas Lord* (The Infallible Silas Lord) in 1938.

Vindry also wrote more than thirty novels, but is best known for his ten locked room mysteries, of which three—*La Maison qui tue* (The House That Kills) in 1932; *La Bête hurlante* (The Howling Beast) and *Le Double Alibi* (The Double Alibi), both in 1934—have already been published by LRI. Two other of his works: *La Fuite des morts*

(The Vanishing Dead) in 1933 and *À travers les murailles* (Through the Walls) in 1937 are also very highly rated.

Pierre Boileau wrote *La Pierre qui tremble* (The Trembling Stone) in 1934; *Le Repos de Bacchus* (Bacchus in Repose), which won the *Grand Prix du Roman d'aventures,* in 1938; his masterpiece *Six Crimes Sans Assassin* (literally Six Crimes Without a Killer) in 1935; writing as Anicot, *Un Assassin au chateau* (A Killer in the Castle) in 1944; and *L'Assassin vient les mains vides* (The Killer Comes Empty-Handed) in 1945. In addition to the aforementioned *La Mort est du voyage,* Narcejac also wrote *L'Assassin de Minuit (*The Midnight Killer*)* in 1945.

Amongst the meteors of the night, in alphabetical order, are:

-Gaston Boca, who wrote four novels between 1933 and 1935, of which two, *L'Ombre sur le jardin* (The Shadow Over the Garden) in1933, and *Les Invités de minuit* (The Seventh Guest) in 1935, are regarded as early classics. The remaining two: *Les Usines de l'effroi* (The Terror Factories) in1934,and *Le Dîner de Mantes* (Dinner at Mantes) in 1935, both have weak solutions.

-Antoine Chollier who wrote *Dossier n°7* (Dossier n°7) in 1946.

-Alexis Gensoul, who wrote *L'Énigma de Tefaha* (The Riddle of Tefaha)*; Gribouille est mort* (Gribouille Is Dead); and—with Charles Garnier—*La Mort vient de nulle part* (Death out of Nowhere), all in 1945, whilst a conscript in the French army.

-Michel Herbert and EugèneWyl, who together wrote *La Maison interdite* (The Forbidden House) in 1932; and *Le Crime derrière la porte* (The Crime Behind the Door) in 1934.

-Maurice Lanteaume, who wrote *Orage sur la Grande Semaine* (Storm Over Festival Week) in 1944, whilst in a German concentration camp; *Trompe-l'œil* (Trompe-l'Œil) in 1946; and *La Treizième balle* (The Thirteenth Bullet) in 1948.

-Roch de Santa-Maria who wrote *Pendu trop court* (Hanged Too Short) in 1937, based on a real-life impossible crime.

Several of the foregoing novels may well be candidates for future LRI publication.

114

PUBLISHERS NOTE

As many readers will know, a couple of years ago Amazon abruptly discontinued the imprint I had been using to publish trade paperbacks, Create Space, together with its choice of templates, forcing myself and others to use the vastly inferior Kindle templates.

With the publication of *Death out of Nowhere* I have stumbled upon another irritating quirk of the Kindle templates: in order for the title to appear on the spine, a book has to contain 130 pages!

Death out of Nowhere is only 112 pages long in tpb format. Not wanting readers to have a blank spine on their bookshelves, and not wanting to add 16 blank pages (in addition to the 2 page Appendix) I needed to find a short story, preferably French, of just the right length to pad the book out.

Even though it had been written in the previous century, "House Call" by Alexandre Dumas was the only one to fit the bill. Subscribers to EQMM, or readers of the LRI anthology *The Realm of the Impossible* will be familiar with the story, which is the very first example of a classic method to create a locked room.

Finally, since no photographs of the authors were available, I inserted one of Rowan Atkinson in the role of Maigret, as a gentle way of making fun of the frustrating proces.

HOUSE CALL

(Chapters 73 and 74 of Alexandre Dumas' 'Les Mohicans de Paris'
(1854))
Mina, Justin's fiancée, has been abducted from her room in Madame
Desmarets' boarding school. Justin's friend Salvator has enlisted the
help of M. Jackal, the mysterious head of the Sûreté.

As for M. Jackal, having learnt from Salvator that Justin was the fiancé, he greeted the young man earnestly and asked if anyone had come in through the garden or the window.

'Nobody, monsieur,' replied Justin.

'Are you sure?'

'Here's the key to the garden.'

'And the key to Mademoiselle Mina's room?'

'The door is locked from the inside.'

'Ah!' said M. Jackal.

And, partaking of an enormous pinch of snuff, he added:

'We'll see about that.'

Then, preceded by Justin, he reached a sort of parlour situated between the courtyard and the garden, from which led the corridor to Mina's room.

Looking around him, he enquired:

'Who is the mistress of this establishment?'

At that moment, Madame Desmarets entered the room.

'Here I am, messieurs,' she said.

'The people I was awaiting from Paris, madame,' said Justin.

'Did you know anything about Mina's disappearance before the arrival of monsieur?' enquired M. Jackal, indicating Justin.

'No, monsieur. I'm not even sure there has been a disappearance,' replied Madame Desmarets in a voice trembling with emotion, 'because we haven't entered her room yet.'

'Rest assured, we'll go in shortly,' said M. Jackal.

And, pulling his glasses down to the end of his nose, he looked over the lenses at Madame Desmarets. The lenses seemed to be there more to hide his eyes than to improve his vision; putting them back in place, he shook his head.

Salvator and Justin stood there, waiting impatiently for the interrogation to continue.

'Would the messieurs care to go into the salon?' asked Madame Desmarets. 'It would be more comfortable there.'

'Thank you, madame,' replied M. Jackal, looking around him again and noting that he had instinctively, like a consummate general, established camp in an excellent position.

'And now, madame,' he continued, 'put your self in the place of a responsible boarding school headmistress who is missing one of her residents, and think very carefully before answering my questions.'

'Oh, monsieur, I couldn't be more painfully affected than I am now,' said Madame Desmarets, wiping away a tear, 'and as for thinking before I answer, that won't be necessary because I will only speak the truth.'

M. Jackal made a small sign of approval and continued.

'At what time do the residents go to bed, madame?'

'At eight o'clock in winter, monsieur.'

'And what about your assistants?'

'At nine o'clock.'

'Do any of them stay up later than the others?'

'Only one.'

'And at what time does she go to bed?'

'Around eleven thirty or midnight.'

'Where does she sleep?'

'On the first floor.'

'Above Mademoiselle Mina's room?'

'No, the person on watch has a room overlooking the dormitory and the street, whereas poor little Mina's room looks out over the garden.'

'And you, Madame. Where do you reside?'

'In a room on the first floor, adjacent to the salon and overlooking the street.'

'So none of your windows overlooks the garden?'

'My bathroom window does.'

'At what time did you go to sleep last night?'

'At about eleven o'clock, roughly.'

'Ah!' said M. Jackal. 'Now we'll do a tour of the house. Come with me Monsieur Salvator. You, Monsieur Justin, stay here and keep madame company.'

One obeyed M. Jackal as one obeyed an army general.

Salavator followed behind. Justin stayed with Madame Desmarets who collapsed on to a chair, sobbing her heart out.

'That woman had nothing to do with it,' said M. Jackal as he went down the front steps and crossed the courtyard to the street door.

'How can you tell?' asked Salvator.

'By the tears' replied M. Jackal. 'The guilty ones tremble but don't cry.'

M. Jackal examined the house.

It was situated on the corner of a street and a deserted, paved alleyway.

M. Jackal set off down the alleyway like a bloodhound on the scent.

To his left, for a length of about fifty feet, rose the garden wall of the boarding school. Above the wall could be seen the tops of trees.

M. Jackal proceeded along the base of the wall with great concentration.

Salvator followed M. Jackal.

The detective indicated the alleyway with a toss of his head.

'Alleys like that are very bad at night. 'They seem to have been designed for abductions and cat burglaries.'

After about twenty five feet, M. Jackal bent down and picked up a small piece of plaster that had been broken off the top of the wall – then another, and a third.

He examined them carefully, then wrapped them in his handkerchief.

Then, picking up a broken piece of tile, he threw it back over the wall, so it landed on the other side.

'Is that where they went over?' asked Salvator.

'We'll find out soon enough,' replied M. Jackal. 'Meanwhile, let's go back inside.'

They found Justin and Madame Desmarets where they had left them.

'Well?' asked Justin.

'We're working on it,' said M. Jackal.

'For mercy's sake, Monsieur, have you found anything, any clues?'

'You're a musician, young man, so you must know the saying: "Don't play faster than the violin." I'm the violin; follow me, but don't get ahead of me... Monsieur Justin, the garden key, if you please.'

The young man handed over the key and, walking along the corridor, said:

'This is the door to Mina's room.'

'Fine, fine. Everything in its turn. We'll go in there later.'

And M. Jackal opened the door to the garden.

He stopped at the entrance, absorbing in one sweeping glance the several places he would examine in more detail later. 'Right!' he said. 'Here we have to exercise precaution and walk as if on eggshells. Follow me if you wish, but in the following order: me first; Monsieur Salvator second; Monsieur Justin third; and Madame Desmarets fourth. Now, fall in behind me!'

It was obvious that M. Jackal was headed towards the portion of the garden wall that he had previously examined from the other side. But, instead of cutting diagonally across the garden, he followed the path that ran along the wall, which obliged him to make a right angle to reach the desired point.

Just before starting out, he cast a glance over his glasses at the window of Mina's room; the shutters were closed.

'Hmm!' he exclaimed, as he set off.

The path, made from yellow sand, offered nothing of interest but, after having travelled roughly twenty five feet after the right-angled turn he stopped and, with a silent laugh, picked up the broken tile he had previously thrown over the wall to act as a point of reference. He pointed out to Salvator the fresh footprint in the adjacent flower-bed.

'Here we are!' he said.

Not only the eyes of Salvator, but also those of Justin and Madame Desmarets followed the direction of M. Jackal's finger.

'So you think the poor child was taken out this way?' asked Salvator.

'There's no doubt about it,' replied the detective.

'My God! My God!' murmured Madame Desmarets, 'an abduction in my boarding school!'

'Monsieur, in heaven's name give us some certitude.'

'Oh, certitude,' exclaimed M. Jackal. 'Look for yourself, my friend, and you'll find it.'

As Justin was looking, M. Jackal, who felt he was on the right track, pulled his snuff-box out of his pocket and gave his nose a mighty dose, all the while examining the ground from under his glasses and Madame Desforets from over them.

'But, monsieur, what exactly do you see?' asked Justin impatiently.

'Those two holes in the ground, connected by a straight line.'

'Don't you recognise the print of a ladder?' Salvator asked Justin.

'Bravo! That's what it is,' said Justin. 'But what's the straight line?'

'Go on, tell him,' said M. Jackal to Salvator.

'It's the bottom rung of the ladder which sank about an inch into the ground because of the humidity of the soil.'

'Now,' continued M. Jackal, 'we have to find out how many men were on the ladder to drive the vertical uprights six inches into the ground and the horizontal rung an inch.'

'Let's examine the footprints,' said Salvator.

'Be careful. Prints can be very confusing. Two men can have walked in the same footprint. There are crafty fellows who have made it a speciality.'

'So what are you going to do?'

'It's very simple.'

Then, turning to the boarding school headmistress, who could no more follow what was happening than if it had been explained in Arab or Sanskrit, he asked:

'Madame, is there a ladder on the premises?'

'There's one that the gardener uses.'

'Where is it?'

'Under the shed, probably.'

'And the shed?'

'Over there.'

'Stay there, I'll fetch it myself.'

M. Jackal lightly jumped about a metre and a half to avoid touching the paths and flower beds where numerous footprints could be seen and which he, following his own method, did not wish to examine until later.

He returned shortly with the ladder.

'Let's make sure of one thing right away,' he said.

He raised the ladder and aligned the uprights with the holes in the flower-bed.

'Good!' he said. 'Here's the first exhibit. This is almost certainly the ladder that was used. The uprights and the holes line up perfectly.'

'But aren't all ladders made to approximately the same dimensions?' asked Salvator.

'This one is slightly wider than normal. The gardener has an apprentice, or a student, or a son, isn't that the case, Madame Desmarets?'

'He has a twelve year old son, monsieur.'

'There we are! His son helps him and he bought a ladder wide enough so that the boy can go up alongside him while he works.'

'Monsieur,' said Justin. 'I beg you, let's get back to Mina.'

'We're getting there, but we're taking a detour.'

'Yes, but the detour is costing us time.'

'My dear sir,' replied the detective, 'in this kind of case time doesn't matter. There are two possibilities: either the fellow who has taken your fiancée has left France and is too far away for us to catch him, or he has hidden her somewhere near Paris, in which case we'll know where he is within three days.'

'Oh, I do so hope you're right, Monsieur Jackal. But you were saying you were about to find out how many men were involved in the abduction.'

'That's exactly what I'm trying to do, monsieur.'

So saying, M. Jackal carried the ladder to a spot roughly one metre from where the first print was found, placed it against the wall, and climbed the first few rungs, stopping at each to assess the depth to which the ladder had sunk into the ground. It never exceeded three inches.

From a position halfway up the ladder, M. Jackal could see the whole garden; he noticed a man on the doorstep of the entrance to the corridor.

'Hello there, friend!' he shouted. Who may you be?'

'I'm Madame Desmarets' gardener,' the man replied.

'Madame,' said M. Jackal, 'please go over there to verify that man's identity and bring him over here, being careful to follow the same path we used.'

Madame Desforets obeyed.

'I tell you, Monsieur Justin – and I repeat, Monsieur Salvator – that woman had nothing to do with the child's abduction.'

Madame Desmarets returned with the gardener, who was quite astonished to find a stranger in his garden, standing on his ladder.

'My friend,' asked M. Jackal, 'did you work in the garden yesterday?'

'No, monsieur. Yesterday was mardi gras, and in an establishment as respectable as Madame Desmarets', one doesn't work on holidays.'

'Fine. And the day before yesterday?'

'Oh, that was lundi gras, and on lundi gras I rest.'

'And the day before that?'

'The day before that was dimanche gras, an even bigger holiday than mardi gras.'

'So that you haven't worked here for the past three days, is that correct?'

'Monsieur,' replied the gardener solemnly, 'I have no wish to be eternally damned.'

'Fine. All I wanted to know was whether your ladder was in the shed for the last three days?'

'My ladder isn't in the shed,' observed the gardener. 'You're standing on it.'

'This man is bursting with intelligence,' commented M. Jackal. 'But I'm quite sure he had nothing to do with the abduction... Please climb the ladder.'

The man looked at Madame Desmarets and read in her eyes that he needed to obey the intruder.

'Do as monsieur tells you,' she said.

The gardener climbed three rungs.

'More,' said M. Jackal.

The gardener continued his climb.

'What do you think?' asked M. Jackal of Salvator.

'It's sinking, but not as far as the rung,' the other replied.

'You can come down, my friend,' said M. Jackal to the gardener.

The man obeyed.

'There, I'm down,' he said.

'I must say,' observed M. Jackal, 'this man doesn't say much, but what he does say is to the point!'

The gardener laughed; he was flattered by what he took to be a compliment.

'Now, my friend,' continued M. Jackal, 'take Madame Desmarets in your arms.'

'Oh!' exclaimed the gardener

'What are you saying, monsieur?' asked Madame Desmarets.

'Take madame in your arms,' repeated M. Jackal.

'I would never dare!' said the gardener.

'And I forbid you to do it, Pierre!' exclaimed the headmistress of the boarding school.

M. Jackal climbed a few rungs, then jumped back down.

'Climb to where I was, my friend,' he said to the gardener.

The gardener went up without difficulty to the rung where M. Jackal had been standing. Meanwhile M. Jackal approached Madame Desmarets, placed one arm around her shoulders and the other around her knees, and lifted her into the air before she had time to realise his intention.

'But monsieur! But monsieur!' cried Madame Desmarets. 'What are you doing?'

'Suppose, madame, that I am in love with you and I carry you off.'

'That's some supposition,' said the gardener, perched on the ladder.

'But monsieur! But monsieur!' repeated Madame Desmarets.

'Rest assured, madame,' continued M. Jackal. 'It's only, as our friend Pierre observed, a supposition.'

And, carrying Madame Desmarets in his arms, he climbed four or five rungs.

'It's going in!' said Salvator, watching the ladder uprights which were pushing further down into the soil.

'Going in as far as the lowest rung?' asked M. Jackal.

'Not quite.'

'Put your foot on the second rung,' said M. Jackal.

Salvator obliged.

'This time,' he said 'it's at exactly the same point as the other.'

'Good,' replied the detective. 'Let's all get down.'

He came down first, placed Madame Desmarets in an upright position, told Pierre to stand where he was on the path, and, pulling the ladder out of the ground, where it had left the same trace as the other, said:

'My dear Monsieur Justin, Madame Desmarets is slightly heavier than Mademoiselle Mina, and I am slightly lighter than the man who carried her, so that all evens out.'

'Which means...?'

'That your fiancée was abducted by three men: two carried her on the ladder while the third kept it in place by putting his foot on it.'

'Ah!' said Justin.

'Now,' continued M. Jackal, 'we shall attempt to establish the identities of the three men.'

'Ah, I understand,' said the gardener. 'One of our residents has been abducted.'

Lowering his glasses, M. Jackal looked long and hard at Pierre, and said:

'Madame Desmarets, don't ever think of getting rid of this lad. He's a glittering jewel of intelligence.'

Then he turned to the gardener and said:

'My friend, you may take your ladder back to where we found it. We shan't need it anymore.'

While the gardener headed off in the direction of the shed, M. Jackal, his glasses pushed up on his forehead and his nose full of snuff, examined the footprints.

Pulling out of his pocket an instrument that seemed half penknife and half pruning knife, he opened one of its nine or ten blades and cut off a small branch with which he started to measure the markings on the ground.

'Observe the tracks,' he said. 'They go from the wall to the window and back. The kidnappers seemed so well informed about the habits of the residents that they didn't feel the need for excessive precautions. But –.' He looked embarrassed. 'But,' he repeated, 'look at the shoes. They are exactly the same length and exactly the same width. Is it possible that, once they were in the garden, only one of them did the job while the others looked on?'

'The shoes are exactly the same length and width,' retorted Salvator. 'But they don't belong to the same foot.'

'Aha! And how can we tell that?'

'From the nails in the sole, which are aligned differently.'

'My goodness, it's true!' exclaimed M. Jackal. 'One of the left shoes has the nails arranged in a triangle. On of our men is a freemason.'

Salvator blushed modestly.

M. Jackal either didn't see it, or pretended not to.

'Plus which,' Salvator continued, 'one of the two men had a limp in his right leg: as you can see, the shoe is worn more on that side than the other.'

'That's true, too,' said the detective. 'Were you ever in the police force?'

'No,' said Salvator. 'But I am – or rather, I was – a hunter.'

'Shush!' said M. Jackal.

'What is it?' asked Salvator.

'There's a third footprint…A very distinctive one, with no resemblance to the flat footed ones we were just looking at. Definitely the foot of a man of the world: an aristocrat, a nobleman or an abbot.'

'A nobleman, I think, Monsieur Jackal.'

'Why must it be a nobleman? I'd rather like to see an abbot mixed up in this business,' said the detective, an admirer of Voltaire.

'I'm afraid you're going to be denied that pleasure.'

'And why is that?'

'Because abbots don't go around on horseback any more, and the man who left this print is a horseman. You can see the spur marks behind the heel of the boot.'

'It's true!' exclaimed M. Jackal. 'Heavens, my dear fellow, you're almost as good as a professional detective.

'That's because I spend a good part of my life observing,' replied Salvator.

'So then help me trace these tracks back to the window.'

'That won't be difficult.'

Sure enough, the tracks of the shoes and boots led straight there.

Justin followed them, hanging on their every word and following their glances. The poor young man was like a miser who had lost a treasure he had guarded jealously for many years, and who, on the brink of finding it again, saw more intelligent souls discover the thieves before he did.

As for Madame Desmarets, she was completely bewildered and stood there stock still, staring into space.

When they arrived at the window, they found the prints had cut deeper into the ground there than elsewhere.

'I was told that you, Madame Desmarets, or you, Monsieur Justin, tried to open Mademoiselle Mimi's door?' asked M. Jackal.

'We did, Monsieur,' they replied in unison.

'And you found it locked with a bolt?'

'It was Mina's habit to lock herself in at night,' replied Madame Desmarets.

'So, they must have got in through the window.'

'Hmm. The shutters seem to be pretty firmly in place,' observed Salvator.

'Oh, it's not difficult to get a shutter open,' said M. Jackal, trying his hand.

'Aha!' he continued. 'Not only is it shut, it's hooked on the inside.'

'Not as easy as you thought?' asked Salvator, slyly.

'You're sure the door's bolted shut?' asked the detective, addressing himself to Justin.

'Oh, yes, Monsieur, I pushed it with all my force.'

'Maybe it was only locked with a key?'

'The upper part of the door sticks to the frame just as much as the middle part.'

'Tut, tut, tut, tut,' said M. Jackal to himself. 'If the shutters were hooked up on the inside and the door was bolted, the people who did this must really know their stuff.'

He shook the shutters again.

'I only know two men capable of getting out of locked doors and windows, and if one wasn't in prison in Brest and the other in

Toulon, I'd say it was either Robichon or Gibassier who pulled this off.'

'So there's a way of getting out through a locked door?' asked Salvator.

'My dear fellow, there's even a way of getting out of a room without a door, as one of my predecessors, the late M. Latude, proved. Luckily, not everyone knows how to do it.'

Then, after partaking generously of snuff, he announced:

'Let's go back inside the house, madame.'

So saying, and without bothering about the niceties of who should go first, he led the way up to the door of Mina's room.

'You obviously must have a duplicate key for every room, madame,' said M. Jackal.

'Yes, but that's not much use if the door is bolted.'

'Fetch it anyway, madame.'

Madame Desmarets disappeared for a short while and returned with the key.

'Here it is,' she said.

M. Jackal inserted the key in the lock and tried to turn it.

'The other key is on the inside, but it hasn't been turned twice.'

Then he added, as if talking to himself:

'That proves the door was locked from the outside.'

'But, if the bolt has been shot,' asked Salvator, 'how did the kidnappers manage to do it from the outside?'

'I'll show you that in a minute, young man: it's Gibassier who devised the method, for which he only got five years hard labour, instead of ten. It was a second offence, but it wasn't considered to be breaking and entering. Now, please find me a locksmith.'

The locksmith duly arrived, armed with a crowbar, and prised the door upwards.

It burst open under the pressure.

Everyone prepared to rush into the room.

M. Jackal, arms outstretched, barred their entry.

'Calm down! Everything hangs on the initial examination. Our investigation is hanging by a thread,' he said with a smirk, as if enjoying a private joke.

Then, going in alone, he examined the lock and the bolt.

He seemed dissatisfied with this first inspection.

Whereupon he removed his glasses – which, apparently, had been the only obstacle to lynx-like vision – and a triumphant smile immediately appeared on his lips as he seized an almost invisible object between thumb and forefinger and brandished it in the air.

'Aha!' he exclaimed happily. 'When I told you our investigation was hanging by a thread … here it is!'

The witnesses were indeed able to make out a thin filament of silk thread, about fifteen centimetres long, which had been trapped between the iron of the bolt and the wood of the door.

'And they were able to close the door with that?' asked Salvator.

'Yes,' replied M. Jackal. 'Except the actual thread was half a metre long, and what you see here is a small piece which broke off and was not noticed.'

The locksmith was watching M. Jackal with astonishment.

'Well,' he said, 'I thought I knew every method of opening and closing a door, but it looks as though I'm just a beginner.'

'I'll be happy to teach you something, my friend,' replied M. Jackal. 'I'll show you how it works. You fold the thread in two – silk is better than cotton, because it's stronger – and you loop it around the knob of the bolt. The thread has to be long enough so that, when the door is closed, the two ends can be gathered from the outside. When you tug on the two ends, the loop tugs on the bolt and the job is done. Except sometimes the thread breaks and gets trapped under the bolt. That's when M. Jackal arrives and says: "If that devil Gibassier wasn't in clink, I would have bet on him." '

'Monsieur Jackal,' said Justin, who clearly had only a faint interest in the subject, 'however important this may be in advancing the progress of science, we really need to get into the room.'

'Quite right, dear Monsieur Justin,' replied the detective.

And everyone entered the room.

'Aha!' exclaimed M. Jackal. 'Footprints from the door to the bed and from the bed to the window.'

Then, taking a quick look at the bed and the adjacent table, he announced:

'So. The child went to bed and read some letters.'

'Oh! My letters,' exclaimed Justin. 'Darling Mina!'

'Then,' continued M. Jackal, 'she blew out the candle; up to

129

that point, everything was all right.'

'How do you know she extinguished the candle herself?' asked Salvator.

'Observe closely: the wick is still curved from being blown out, and to judge from the shape of the curve, the gust of air came from the direction of the bed. Let's go back to the footprints, please; Monsieur Salvator, look at this one with your hunter's eyes.'

Salvator bent down.

'Ah! Ah!' he exclaimed. 'Here's something new: a woman's foot!'

'What did I tell you, Monsieur Salvator? "Cherchez la femme!" As you say, a woman's foot…And, upon my word, a resolute woman, not walking on tiptoe, but pressing firmly on the sole and the heel.'

'Yes,' replied Salvator, 'and a woman concerned about her appearance. She kept to the garden paths, so as not to dirty her boots; notice how the print is traced in yellow sand without any hint of mud.'

'Monsieur Salvator, Monsieur Salvator,' exclaimed the detective. 'What a pity you chose your current profession! You can be my aide de camp anytime you want. Don't move!'

M. Jackal left the room, went down into the garden, walked along the sandy path to the foot of the ladder, and returned.

'That's it,' he said. 'The woman left the house, followed the path, stopped at the ladder, and retraced her steps. Now I'm going to tell you what happened. I couldn't be more sure if I'd seen it with my own eyes.'

Everyone listened attentively.

'Mademoiselle Mina came into the house at the usual hour, very sad but calm; she went to bed – look, the bed has hardly been slept in! – and read some letters. She cried while reading them -- look at her handkerchief: it's crumpled like that of someone who's been crying…'

'Oh! Give it to me! Give it to me!' exclaimed Justin.

And, without waiting for M. Jackal to give it to him, he picked it up and pressed it to his lips.

'So she went to bed,' continued M. Jackal, 'she read, and she cried. But, because you can't read if you can't cry any more, she felt the need to sleep and blew out the candle. Did she sleep, or didn't she? It doesn't matter. However, once the candle was out, this is what happened. Someone knocked at the door –.'

'Who, monsieur?' asked Madame Desmarets.

'Ah! You want to know more than I do myself, dear madame! Who? Maybe I'll be able to tell you shortly. The woman, in any case.'

'The woman?' murmured Madame Desmarets.

'The wife, the daughter, the mother: when I say woman, I'm referring to the species, not to anyone in particular. So the woman knocked on the door, and Mina got up and opened it.'

'But why would Mina open the door without knowing who was knocking?' asked Madame Desmarets.

'Who told you she didn't know who it was?'

'She wouldn't have opened it to an enemy.'

'No, but to a friend?...Ah, Madame Desmarets, am I to be the one to reveal to you that in boarding schools there are friends who are also terrible enemies? So Mina opened the door to her friend. Standing behind this friend was the young man in riding boots and stirrups. And standing behind the young man in riding boots and stirrups was the man with the triangular pattern of nails in his soles. How did little Mina sleep?'

'I don't understand,' said Madame Desmarets, to whom the question was addressed.

'I meant: what clothes did she wear at night?'

'In winter she wore a shirt and a large dressing-gown.'

'Good! So they stuffed a handkerchief in her mouth, wrapped her in a shawl or a bedcover – look there at the foot of the bed, her stockings and shoes; and on the chair, her dress and petticoat – and they took her out through the window like that.'

'Through the window?' asked Justin. 'Why not through the door?'

'Because they would have had to go along the corridor and someone may have heard them. In any case, it was simpler for the two men in the room to hand the child over to the man waiting in the garden. Come to think of it, the fact that the shutters and windows were so securely shut is further proof that she was taken out that way and that she didn't go of her own free will.'

M. Jackal indicated where a large piece had been torn out of the muslin curtain by a hand that had grabbed hold of it.

'So that's what happened. The child was taken out through the window, and then passed over the wall. After that, the person still left on the premises put the ladder back in the shed, went back into the house, locked the windows and shutters on the inside, looped a silk thread around the bolt knob, closed the door, pulled on the thread, and went peacefully to bed.'

'But while she was going in and out of the dormitory she must have been seen.'

'Have you any other residents occupying their own room like Mademoiselle Mina?'

'Only one.'

'Then she's the one who carried it out. My dear Monsieur Salvator, we've found the woman!'

'What? You think it's Mina's friend who is the cause of all this?'

'I didn't say the cause, I said the accomplice.'

'Suzanne!' exclaimed Madame Desmarets.

'Madame,' said Justin, 'Believe me, it must be the case.'

'But what put that idea in your head, monsieur?'

'The dislike I felt for that young woman the first time I saw her. Oh, madame! It was like a premonition that something awful would happen because of her. As soon as monsieur started talking about a woman,' continued Justin, indicating M. Jackal, 'I thought of her. I didn't dare accuse her, but I suspected her. For heaven's sake, monsieur, bring her here and confront her.'

'No,' replied M. Jackal. 'Let's not bring her here, let's go to her. Madame, please lead us to the young woman's room.'

Madame Desmarets who, in the face of the relentless M. Jackal, had lost all will to resist, went ahead wordlessly and pointed the way.

The room was situated on the first floor at the end of the corridor.

'Knock on the door, madame,' instructed M. Jackal.

Madame Desmarets knocked, but there was no reply.

'She may be on the eleven o'clock break,' said Madame Desmarets. 'Should I call her?'

'No,' replied M. Jackal. 'Let's look at her room first.'

'There's no key in the door.'

'But you have duplicate keys for all the doors. Isn't that what you told me?'

'Yes, monsieur.'

'Well then, go and find the spare key for Mademoiselle Suzanne's room, and if you happen to see her, not a word about what we've found. On your head be it.'

Madame Desmarets indicated that they could count on her discretion and went downstairs. A few seconds later she returned with the key, which she handed to M. Jackal.

The door was opened.

'Messieurs,' said M. Jackal. 'Wait for me in the corridor. Madame Desmarets and I will make the inspection.'

The two of them went in.

'There,' said Madame Desmarets, indicating a closet.

M. Jackal opened the door and found a pair of blue sapphire boots on a shelf inside. He inspected the sole, which had traces of the yellow sand from the garden path along its entire length.

'Do the residents go into the orchard?' he asked Madame Desmarets.

'No, Monsieur,' came the reply. 'The orchard, which overlooks a deserted alleyway, is not locked, but is strictly out of bounds.'

'That's good,' said M. Jackal, putting the boots back in their place. 'I know what I wanted to know. Now, where do you think Mademoiselle Suzanne is at this moment?'

'In all likelihood, she's in the playground.'

'And which room in your establishment overlooks the playground?'

'The salon.'

'Then let's go to the salon, Madame.'

So saying, he walked out of Mademoiselle Suzanne's room, leaving Madame Desmarets to lock the door.

'Well?' asked Salvator and Justin in unison.

'Well,' replied M. Jackal partaking of a huge pinch of snuff. 'I think we've found the woman!'